FROST

GALAXY ALIEN MAIL ORDER BRIDES: A QURILIXEN WORLD NOVELLA

MICHELLE M. PILLOW

MICHELLE M. PILLOW® - MICHELLEPILLOW.COM

First Electronic Printing Sept 2018

Published by The Raven Books LLC

ISBN 978-1-62501-219-7

This novel is a work of fiction. Any and all characters, events, and places are of the author's imagination and should not be confused with fact. Any resemblance to persons, living or dead, or events or places is merely coincidence.

ABOUT THE BOOK

FROST

All he wanted was a little adventure and maybe to find a wife on Earth. What he got was a hell of a lot more than this alpha alien bargained for.

NYT Bestselling Author, Michelle M. Pillow, is back with a brand new sci fi alien romance adventure.

Alpha male alien Edur (aka Frost Chaos) will do anything to escape his ice tundra of a home planet. He'll even convince his brothers to jump onboard a bride procurement spaceship bound for Earth... which to be honest he should have vetted a little better.

Galaxy Brides promises a land of untold beauties just waiting for strong alien men to come and abduct them away.

Galaxy Brides promises a lot of things they can't deliver.

Galaxy Brides should maybe not be in business.

Journalist Meg Taylor had no problem leaving her big city life behind to come home to care for her sick father, but she does miss the excitement of chasing a story. When rumors of a blue hockey player surface in her small town, she can't resist. But following Frost home will give her more story than she bargained for--dangerous mercenaries, spaceships, intrigue, and a sexy blue-skinned alien looking for more than a one night stand.

WELCOME TO QURILIXEN

QURILIXEN WORLD NOVELS

Dragon Lords Series

Barbarian Prince

Perfect Prince

Dark Prince

Warrior Prince

His Highness The Duke

The Stubborn Lord

The Reluctant Lord

The Impatient Lord

The Dragon's Queen

Lords of the Var Series

The Savage King

The Playful Prince

The Bound Prince

The Rogue Prince

The Pirate Prince

Captured by a Dragon-Shifter Series

Determined Prince

Rebellious Prince

Stranded with the Cajun

Hunted by the Dragon

Mischievous Prince

Headstrong Prince

Space Lords Series

His Frost Maiden

His Fire Maiden

His Metal Maiden

His Earth Maiden

His Woodland Maiden

Dynasty Lords Series

Seduction of the Phoenix

Temptation of the Butterfly

To learn more about the Qurilixen World series of books and to stay up to date on the latest book list visit www.MichellePillow.com

AUTHOR UPDATES

To stay informed about when a new book in the series installments is released, sign up for updates:

michellepillow.com/author-updates

WELCOME TO GALAXY BRIDES

A NOTE FROM THE AUTHOR

Dear Readers,

For those of you familiar with my bestselling series, Dragon Lords and Lords of the Var, you've already been introduced to the Galaxy Brides Corporation and the services they offer lonely men and women of the future.

What you might not have known is that Galaxy Brides (formerly known as "Galaxy Alien Mail Order Brides") dabbled in taking grooms to destinations instead of bring brides to the grooms. Namely, they tried taking the guys to Earth.

Unfortunately, the experiment didn't last long. The corporation found the alien males a little too hard to control once they landed on our surface, and the local females to be just as strong-willed.

I hope you have as much fun reading this series as I've had writing it!

Happy Reading!
Michelle M. Pillow

GALAXY ALIEN MAIL ORDER BRIDES

HAVE YOU READ THEM ALL?

Spark
Flame
Blaze
Ice
Frost
Snow

To the Pillow Fighter Fan Club
A big thanks to dedicated readers like you willing to help spread the word about the books they love.
Thank you!

PRAISE FOR MICHELLE M. PILLOW

What readers are saying about the
Galaxy Alien Mail Order Brides series...

5 Stars! "Hysterically funny, spicy and sweet."

5 Stars! "One of the best alien romance stories I have read!"

5 Stars! "A must read to all who enjoy alien hotties!"

5 Stars! "Action, Intrigue, and humor with a happy ever afters!"

5 Stars! "Funny, adventurous, and romantic. The male aliens are funny as all get out!"

1

PROLOGUE

Planet of Sintaz

Edur peered hopefully at the holographic chip that the short, large-headed being slipped into his hand. Peeks of tough yellow skin showed wherever the alien's garments didn't cover, which wasn't saying much since his clothes covered him practically everywhere. Though Edur wasn't sure what manner of alien this "Bob" was, the man had assured him that the disc contained, "everything a lonely alien man needs to make his dreams come true."

Okay, actually, thanks to the bad translators that often got the nuances of his Sintazian language wrong, Bob had said, "everything a lost blue monster requires to make wishes into nourishing soup," but Edur got the gist of what he meant. They had enough run-ins with aliens coming to their ice planet that he'd become adept at interpreting the mechanical translators.

"Wishes into soup," Edur said softly as he held the disc up to the light.

"Wishes into nourishing soup." Bob nodded. He wore a puffy jacket that read "Galaxy Alien Mail Order Brides" in the Old Star language over his chest. Though he smiled, the poor guy looked nearly frozen through and today wasn't even a cold one for the ice tundra he'd landed on. That very reason was why it was impossible to get people to stay on the planet. Even the Sintazians had been slowly migrating off world. Hauling cargo in a refrigerated spaceship held more promise than hunting bearguars and hairy bellaphants to keep from starving during the worst of the ice storms.

Edur stood shirtless in only boots and pants and didn't need a coat. He was used to the temperature. It was the heat that sometimes gave him a problem.

Sintaz did not provide an easy life. It was hard, lonely, isolated, and rather dull. Edur lived with his two brothers. He loved them, but there were times he wished he had someone else to talk to. Even if that someone was the strange Bob alien speaking to him in translator riddles.

Bob said his foreign words into his translating device, only to have it say, "Should you need to undertake the capture of a woman journey, please select the ghost button at the end of the device recording to alert us of the connected ones' favorable reception. Space credits will be withdrawn from your shower."

That one took Edur a moment to figure out. If he and his brothers' answer was yes, push the button to be taken to women?

"We will return to capture you in star dates on the button."

Push the button and they'll come back on the date shown. Got it. Simple enough.

"Women?" Edur lifted the holo-disc to clarify. If they paid for this trip and ended up with actual soup, he'd be angry. But, if it was women, he had to admit there was a substantial part of him that wanted to say yes right then and there.

His oldest brother, Izotz, would never go for this. If Izotz said no, then Tushar would not come either. If they didn't come, then he would have to stay as well. He could never leave his brothers behind.

Bob did a series of enthusiastic gestures. One of which Edur recognized as an affirmation. "Multiple eager, jolly-making women waiting for strong blue monsters to abduct them from their homes."

"For me?" Edur pointed at his chest. "And my brothers?"

Bob again went through his small routine to agree.

Not really sure what he was doing, Edur repeated some of the gestures back to him. Bob stood still as if he didn't know how to react.

"Thank you, I will look at this and discuss it with my family," Edur said, indicating he would take the device and look at it.

Bob answered, and the translator said, "No, I do not require the devouring of waste. I must," *something indecipherable,* "spaceship."

Bob reached out his covered hand.

This was a gesture he'd seen before. Edur mimicked the movement, stretching his bare blue hand forward to hover a few inches away. Bob touched his hand, and Edur stiffened. A soft green glow came from beneath Bob's glove, showing through the material. The touch was brief and tingling, and when Bob released him, he turned to trudge through the thick snow drift back to his ship.

An expanse of ice and snow created the entire landscape of an unforgiving planet. Sometimes the snow was so deep it could swallow a man whole. Other times, it was slick, and they had to slide rather than walk, only to be careful not to slide right off the side of a cliff. Then there were those times when the glassy surface was deceiving, and one false step would drop them into a ravine so vast they'd be killed on impact.

Snow drifts and ice cliffs, that was Sintaz. Theirs was not an easy life, but it was the only life they had known. Edur wanted more. He wanted adventure. He wanted romance. He wanted someone to talk to who wasn't his brothers. He knew all of Tushar and Izotz's stories because he'd been there for most of them and the rest he'd heard a million times.

Edur watched Bob struggle. He thought about lifting the little guy and carrying him to the ship but knew that would be considered inappropriate. It was clear no one had prepared these aliens to land on Sintaz. They'd picked the worst location to set down. Snow piled up the sides of the craft.

The metal hull was probably coated with ice. The heat would have melted the snow when it landed, and the temperature would have frozen the moisture back onto it. Legend said there were hundreds if not thousands of alien spaceships buried beneath the planet's surface, either crash-landed or having become trapped in ice.

Like all Sintazians, Edur's blue skin was biologically adapted to the elements, and he did not need a snowsuit most days, but few non-native aliens could take the weather. He would never admit the truth of wanting to leave to his brothers. They would not take that statement well, not after so many had already gone, leaving them virtually isolated.

Edur was jealous of the others who'd left on cargo ships, or with the ESC scientific research teams. The constant ice and snow tired him. He wanted excitement. He wanted new stories to tell, ones that didn't include deadly ice storms and tracking bellaphants for food.

Edur watched to make sure Bob reached his destination. The alien stumbled into his ship, and the loading platform creaked as it tried to retract behind him. With some effort, the metal broke away and pulled back into the vessel.

Edur placed the holographic disc in his hand and activated it. A transparent image lifted from his palm to float before him. It was of a peculiar planet with patches of brown surrounded by blue. There were swirls of white clouds hovering over the globe.

A soft alien voice spoke, only to be overpowered by the louder, deep male voice programmed into the translator, "Is yours one of the many stagnant civilizations without enough women to produce offspring?"

Edur nodded. "Yes, we are."

"Do you come from a monogamist culture with no one to marry? Or a polygamist culture in need of more food makers? Are you lonely and looking to reassign your assets? What if we told you there is a planet whose name is called Earth that could solution all your needs? Would you be jolly? Earth has women they are willing to share. So, join us for jolly-making on Earth, where all your humanoid female fantasies can become digestible food."

At that he frowned a little and hoped it was a mistranslation.

"Earth has a breathable sky, food you can put in your heart, and..." The translator blipped and began streaming a rapid succession of alien words, before resuming, "officially discovered life forms not of their own planet but are humanoid compactible and ready for travel to their new homes. Upon mate selection, all necessary papers will be given to the Earth government and transport will be taken upon us, as you leave the planet with your new food makers we will provide the transport."

"Will you provide the transport?" Edur muttered to himself. He wondered how much he was missing because of the lousy translation. Surely the original message didn't keep repeating itself.

"Those wishing to stay on Earth will be provided with manly identity," the translator promised.

Edur glanced up as the ship's engines initiated. He took a few steps back and paused the recording so it wouldn't be drowned out by the sounds of takeoff.

The ship trembled as if struggling. Edur let loose a small laugh. The craft jerked a few times before finally managing to break free of the planet's surface. When it lifted from the ground, a giant chunk of ice clung to its underbelly and weighed it down.

As the noise subsided, he resumed watching the hologram. It showed what Earth women looked like as a humanoid figure appeared, floating in rotation so he could get a look at her from all angles. She had the right amount of legs and arms. That was a plus. Though, there were two mounds of flesh on her chest that Sintazian women did not have. That was peculiar and yet fascinating.

"Option one." The first woman wore tight clothes and had long brown hair that fell down her back. She was also a very alien shade of non-blue.

"Option two." The second woman wore a sparkly gown and had lighter-colored hair piled high on her head. Without thinking, Edur touched one of her mounds of flesh. The image distorted a little.

"Option three." The third woman wore black-rimmed eye protectors. He assumed she must be an adventurer of some sort. She opened a rectangular device containing alien words and her lips moved as if she recited an incantation. Her hair was black, like his people's. That was something.

"Option four." A redhead exhaled smoke. Her black clothes clung to her curves like a second skin. He found that look very intriguing. In fact, all of the women were intriguing.

"Option five." The woman was naked except for two strips of clothing over her chest and hips. Her hair came in two if not three colors. The strange skin tone was clearly all over their bodies. Edur again poked at one of the soft globes on the image's chest, wondering what they felt like.

He waited for an option six, but nothing appeared.

"Such variety," he said to himself in surprise. He felt his body vibrate as he became excited. Earth did apparently have many women to choose from. He would like very much to put himself into one of them and vibrate to completion.

Metal groaned, and he glanced up in time to see a mass of ice coming straight for him.

He fisted the holographic disc and ran, diving onto the ground to slide out of the projectile's way. As the ice from the ship made an impact, it shattered, sending shards raining over him. The sharp edges cut his naked back, and he grunted at the discomfort.

"I hate this place," Edur grumbled. He opened his hand as he lay on his stomach. The hologram appeared at an angle. A circular image floated with a star date inscribed on it. He had enough space credits to pay for the trip. Really, what else was he going to do with them? He didn't need convincing as he pushed it and marked passage for three people. "Anywhere but here."

Edur smiled as he stood up from the ground. Excitement filled him as he hurried home toward the ice hut. He couldn't wait to tell his brothers what he'd done. With that thought, his steps faltered, and he tripped.

Oh no.

He had to tell his brothers.

He might convince Tushar but Izotz...

Izotz was the oldest of the three. After they lost their parents to an ice storm, Izotz took responsibility for the family. It was because of him that none of them had left the planet with the others. He wasn't sure he could get Izotz on a ship when the time came.

As much as he wanted to leave, his brothers came first. If Izotz didn't go, Edur would stay as well. If he was to take a solo trip, and something happened while he was away, he would never forgive himself.

"What did the alien ship want?" Tushar came from inside the ice hut. He glanced around the barren landscape, his eyes stopping on the chunks of ice that had fallen from the sky. Almost resignedly, he said, "It's warm today. Izotz will want to hunt for the winter supply."

"Merchants," Edur said, answering Tushar's question. He rolled the disc in his palm with his fingers.

"Snowsuits or heat dispensers?" Tushar chuckled, guessing the two most common items aliens tried to sell them.

"Women," Edur answered. "They want to marry us off."

Tushar laughed harder, obviously thinking he'd made a joke. "Wouldn't that be something, a bridal procurement agency landing here for the three of us? They'd probably try to pair us with those hairy aliens we saw with the ESC. Who else could withstand our temperatures?"

"Or Izotz's cooking," Edur added.

The brothers laughed.

"What were they selling?" Tushar asked

again. They didn't get many visitors, so a landing spaceship always broke up the tedium of the day.

"Women," Edur repeated.

"No, really." Tushar crossed his arms over his chest. "Why won't you tell me?"

Edur opened his fist and handed his brother the holo-disc. "They are looking to take men to Earth for mating."

"What is Earth?" Tushar eyed the disc without turning it on.

"A planet with many women." Edur took a deep breath and looked away. "It sounds like the women are expecting to be abducted and are even excited about it."

"What did you do?" Tushar placed a fist on Edur's shoulder, as if sensing his guilt.

"I signed us up to go," admitted Edur. "They took my space credits. I do not think I can get them back."

Tushar didn't move for a long while. Finally, he let his hand drop to his side. He glanced at the doors to the hut. "You signed our brother up for a marriage trip? Izotz? On a spaceship? To this *Erd* place?"

"Will you help me convince him of the idea?" Edur asked.

Tushar laughed and shook his head in denial. "No."

"Will *you* go?"

"It depends on how hairy these *Erd* brides are." Tushar laughed harder. "But first, I want to see you tell Izotz he's to be married to an off-world hairy alien. He will drop you down an ice crevice."

"The women are not hairy," Edur insisted. "They are..."

He thought of the soft chest globes.

Edur reached over to start the holographic sales pitch. The planet appeared, rotating as it hovered over Tushar's hand.

"It looks...warm," Tushar said.

"Is yours one of the many stagnant civilizations without enough women to produce offspring? Do you come from a monogamist culture with no one to marry? Or a polygamist culture in need of more food makers? Are you lonely and looking to reassign your assets? What if we told you there is a planet whose name is called Earth..."

2

November, Northern Minnesota,
Several Earth Months Later...

Earth was not as Galaxy Alien Mail Order Brides had described.

It was not safe.

It was not an easy place to meet women.

It was not jolly-making.

Galaxy Brides had promised a land of untold beauties who eagerly awaited strong alien men to come and abduct them away. In reality, no one was waiting to be abducted, and he highly doubted the Earth government knew an alien spacecraft was landing to pick up its citizens.

The ship had dropped them off in the dark of

night in a remote location and promptly took off minutes before a group of mercenary soldiers came to capture them. They managed to apprehend Izotz and locked him in a cage. Instead of coming back to help, Galaxy Brides had left them to fend for themselves.

This was not the trip Edur had paid for.

Galaxy Brides promised them a lot of things they could not deliver.

Galaxy Brides should maybe not be in business.

As hard as Edur tried to hold on to the Sintazian language, if he didn't concentrate, all of his thoughts came in English. The corporation had filled their head with the Earth language using a brain upload. Well, Izotz was first given a not-so-lovely dialect of Venimice before the crew realized they had the wrong file. Now Izotz could gurgle-speak with the best of them. A skill he'd never use.

Galaxy Brides then gave the brothers new identities. Edur's Earth name was now Frost Chaos. Izotz was Ice Storm Chaos, and Tushar was called Snow Chaos. It was the one thing Galaxy Brides had done right. The names were what humans would call, "badass." Frost didn't understand how having a bad ass was a good thing, but he'd only been on Earth for a few months.

Frost still remembered that moment when he'd turned around to find masked men had overtaken Ice. Snow had tried to go back, but he'd stopped him. There were too many humans and saving one brother would be hard enough, let alone two. So, instead, Frost used the emergency signal that the Galaxy Brides aliens had given him to summon the ship back. The inept aliens had taken a long time to respond. When they did, Frost took Gary hostage and held him until they found Ice. It seemed only fair. His brother was imprisoned, why not one of Galaxy Brides' employees? Gary's excuse for the delay was that they'd thought the beacon was activated in error.

Ice's now-wife had subsequently freed him from his cage. Elle worked for the Milano Foundation that had captured Ice, but at the time, she'd thought aliens weren't real, and the mercenary job was a joke that happened to pay well. Ice and Elle's pairing had been far from easy. The Milano Foundation would stop at nothing to capture three intergalactic visitors.

As long as they were on Earth, the brothers would be in hiding.

The snow in Minnesota blanketed the area but could not hide the fact he was not home. Instead of ice cliffs, there were trees resting for the winter. Where there should be an icy tundra slick from centuries of being packed down, there were now valleys with dots of green poking through the white. Whereas the humans bundled up in clothes in such weather, Frost and his brothers found the winter to be warm and did not need a heavy jacket or long pants. In fact, he'd be fine walking around naked.

It was not lost on Frost that it had been his idea to look for women, and now he wanted to leave. At least Ice had found a bride. The trip wasn't a complete waste of space credits.

"The newest face to amateur Voyageurs hockey is one you can't miss. Painted in a signature blue, the winger they call Chaos has literally taken the small town of Rumble by storm in only a few games."

Frost didn't lift his eyes as his brother threw the newspaper down on the table. He sat in the kitchen of the guesthouse they lived in, overlooking the snowy scene outside. Elle had led them to the Earth sanctuary in Voyageurs National Park. Her parents owned the property and had given them refuge. The kitchen opened to the large living room. A hallway led back to a bedroom suite where Ice stayed with his wife. Frost's and Snow's rooms were on the second level.

Ice placed his finger on the page. His brother's human-colored flesh was hard to get used to, especially when compared to Frost's blue. "Where did this mystery man come from? It's like he fell from the stars right onto the rink."

Frost gave his brother a hopeful smile. "I think I found a way to blend in. Nice, huh?"

Ice and Snow could intermingle with the humans much easier by using the mystical baby aspirin to change their skin tones. Frost's body had rejected the chemical, and he remained the only genuine blue man on Earth. There was a group of performers who covered themselves in blue, and a condition where human skin tinted when they consumed too much silver, but those cases were hardly the same.

To leave the country sanctuary, Frost had needed to figure out a way to blend in, and that is what he did.

Sort of.

Ice stood for a long moment, breathing hard. He did that when he was upset and thinking of something to say. "You think this is nice?"

"Not nice?" Frost frowned. "You said if I found a way to hide who I was then I could meet women. The females like a man who can play sports. Really, it's like a child's game, slipping around on the ice after a small black disc, but it is fun, and I am good at it."

Ice sat at the table across from him. Earth homes were a series of strange square rooms butted up against each other with frilly decorations hanging on the walls and over windows. Some things were the same—tables and bowls and doors, for the most part—but much was different enough to be alien. Every waking moment was a reminder that he was a stranger on this planet and could not fit in like his brothers.

"I had to think of something," Frost said when Ice didn't respond. "I have little time to meet a woman. Galaxy Brides is coming back in a few months to give whoever is leaving a ride back."

When his brother finally spoke, his words were calmer than Frost expected. "So you have changed your mind and have decided to return to Sintaz?"

"What other decision is there for me? Hockey was the best idea I could come up with." Frost shook his blue arm. "Look at me."

"If I were honest, I would rather look at you than at me. I don't recognize myself." Ice lifted his hands. "These don't look like my hands." He touched his arm where the dark blue markings had turned black. "People think I have a tattoo now, not a birthmark."

Frost touched his arm where his birthmark swirled up onto his shoulder, peeking out from the short sleeve of the t-shirt Elle had given him to wear. The color was a darker blue compared the lighter blue of his skin.

"You know that life for a human woman on Sintaz would not be a pleasant one," Ice said. "If you were to meet a woman and take her to our home world, she would be trapped much of the time indoors and bundled in an ESC snowsuit for the rest of it. You would be asking her to live a lonely existence. These humans are social creatures. When I go with Elle to the store to procure food, the women all stop and talk to each other, sometimes for minutes, about nothing."

"Surely not nothing," Frost countered.

Ice sighed. "The last conversation lasted for sixteen Earth minutes and was about a spray for the hair. Two times before that had lasted eleven Earth minutes and was about their face paint holding up in the wetter weather."

"They call it makeup," Frost corrected. "Elle tried painting it on me to hide my skin. It didn't work. I looked worse than a Kintok sex slave."

Ice gave a little chuckle at the analogy. "It did look bad."

"You did not see it," countered Frost.

"We did." Ice laughed harder. "Snow and I were peeking in through the window after Elle locked us out of the room."

Frost lifted the newspaper and threw it at his brother's head. Ice swatted it away and continued to laugh.

"I'm glad you find amusement in this," Frost said.

"No, not in this, but in your face painting," Ice corrected. His smile fell a little. "I don't want you to go back to Sintaz. I want you to stay here."

Oh, how roles had changed. Izotz had not wanted to come, and now he didn't want to leave.

"I can't stay." Frost turned to gaze out of the

window. "I will never fit in here. If I cannot hide, then I am a danger to all of you. A blue man on Earth stands out."

"I can't go back with you because of Elle," Ice insisted. "How will you survive the winter months alone?"

"Has Snow decided he is staying?" Frost watched his brother's reflection in the window. The difference in their appearances was unmistakable.

"He has not said, but I do not want him to leave either." Ice leaned forward and put his fist against Frost's arm. "There must be something else you can take to change your skin. If we ask Galaxy Brides—"

"Don't you think that was one of the many conversations I had with Gary as I held him hostage to force Galaxy Brides to find you?"

It would seem Elle was the exception to women on Earth. She had claimed Ice as her mate while his skin was blue.

Elle's mother knew the truth and looked at him with concern in her gaze—and not exactly concern for Frost. She would stare at his birthmark and his face, especially when Frost pretended not to be paying attention. It didn't matter how nice he tried to be to her. It was close to the reaction he'd gotten when he'd ventured downtown in nearby Rumble. It was only after he'd joined a hockey game that he'd been accepted...and that was only by the men playing. They thought his face was a tattoo since the rest of him had been hidden by human winter clothes. By his accented words, they assumed it was an exotic tribal custom—whatever that meant.

"I have tried to find a place here," Frost admitted. "But if my playing hockey is of concern, then I have nothing. They are the only ones who have accepted me and think my blue face is either a tattoo or a gimmick. I am fully clothed. I hide as much as I can."

"Our hiding place here is precarious at best. If the Milano Foundation scientists see this article, if they became curious enough to look..." Ice seemed to struggle with his words.

Frost nodded in understanding. "Milano will not only come for us, but they will come for Elle and possibly her family." He would never put them in danger. "I did not know they would write about it. They are not even in a thing called a big league. I will go tonight and tell the team that I am not returning, so they do not try to find me. I have seen those missing persons on television. I do not want to see my face on there."

Ice picked the newspaper off the floor and set it on the table. In Sintazian, he said, "Thank you for your understanding. For what it is worth, the story is a good one. Well done, Edur."

Elle appeared from the hallway leading to the room she shared with Ice, signifying why his brother had changed his language to compliment him about playing. Frost imagined Elle would be upset about possible exposure. He couldn't blame her. She risked much hiding them.

"I did not think it would cause concern. I will take care of this now." Frost stood. He nodded at Elle. "There will be no more articles about me. I promise. It was not my wish to upset you."

3

Finally. Something of human interest happening in Rumble worth writing about.

Meg Taylor tapped her finger on the newspaper article about a blue man playing hockey. There was only a picture of the team on the ice, but if it was true, then there might be something as to the reason for the blue. And, maybe, just maybe, she could spin something out of it. Anything had to be better than writing ad copy and blog articles for internet businesses. Although, her piece about the correct material to use for different plumbing jobs was quite riveting...if you were a finicky homeowner hiring a plumber to install new pipes.

There was nothing wrong with Rumble, as a

town—the people were friendly, the streets were clean, the bars closed at midnight, and there was hardly any trouble. But what made the town "nice" also made it boring as hell.

There was a reason she'd left.

There was also a reason she had come back three years ago.

Meg glanced up to where her father, Jerry, sat in front of the television in his wheelchair. He'd been a lifelong smoker, and that vice had finally caught up with him. The wheelchair was from a car accident when she was in elementary school. He could stand and walk short distances with a cane but had limited mobility from the waist down. Their main concern started as emphysema and had led to the diagnosis of chronic obstructive pulmonary disease, COPD. He would use an oxygen tank for the rest of his life.

At first, her father had tried to downplay his poor health, not wanting to upset her big-city life. But, being a journalist, she had done her research. She'd called his doctor and, since they'd signed a paper stating she could access his medical records, Dr. Alexakis had filled her in. The doctor insisted Jerry shouldn't be living alone and had suggested she consider either hiring him a full-time health care aide or prepare him for eventually going into a nursing home. Since her mother was no longer with them, he had no one else.

Meg had sold what she could, said goodbye to her budding career, told the man she was casually dating they were over, and moved home from Chicago within a week. She didn't regret the decision. Not for a second. This is what people did for family. A fancy job could never take the place of her father's life. There would be other jobs.

That also didn't mean her life had to stop. Meg reached for a notepad and wrote, "*Who are you? Why the color blue? Where from? When did you move here? What brought you here? How do you apply the color or is it a tattoo? Does it wash off easily?*"

"I know that expression."

Meg glanced up to see her father studying her. She hadn't heard him come toward the table. His short dark hair stuck up on the side as if he'd been scratching his head. He did that often. "You have an idea, don't you?"

Meg nodded. "Blue hockey player in town."

"Ah, interesting." Her father nodded. He'd always been one of her greatest supporters. "Going to hunt him down and make him talk?"

"Something like that," she laughed. "Are you all right here by yourself? Do you need anything? I have my phone and will drop whatever I'm—"

"Gah, no, go." He waved his hand toward the door. "Jenny is stopping by later to visit. I'll be fine."

"I see." Meg nodded. Jenny Mirani was a kind woman, who had a stereotypical die-hard hippie fondness for patchouli and a fashion sense that was firmly stuck in the 1960s and '70s. The woman also had a heart of gold and never failed to check on Meg's father. "You don't need your daughter hanging around as you put the moves on Ms. Mirani."

"You're not too old to ground," her father warned. "And for the record, Jenny puts the moves on me. What can I say? I'm a catch."

"Yes, you are, Dad." She stood and leaned to kiss him on the head. They were close, but she didn't want to hear the details of her father's dating life. She highly suspected that someday soon, her father would announce his engagement to the woman. "Don't let Ms. Mirani look in the garage freezer. She's brought over so many casseroles that I've started hiding them out there.

Just ask her to put this one in the oven for tonight."

"How do you know she'll bring me a casserole?"

Meg laughed as she grabbed her coat and oversized messenger bag that doubled as a camera bag and purse. Instead of taking her wallet, she shoved some cash into her pocket. "It doesn't take a trained journalist to deduce Ms. Mirani will try to feed us."

"And it doesn't take a trained father to know you're about to forget your notepad and cellphone."

"Oh, yes, thank you." She grabbed them off the table and shoved the items in her bag. "Wish me luck."

"A good hunter doesn't need luck. Knock 'em dead, kiddo. Get your story."

She gave him a big smile. "Have fun on your date tonight. I'll find a place to crash, so don't wait up."

4

"I MUST LEAVE," FROST STATED, KEEPING HIS head down as he spoke to the captain of the Voyageurs hockey team. Skates swished in steady rhythms on the rectangular ice rink as the team practiced. Soaring over the ice was the only time he'd felt like he had a piece of home. The competition just made it even more enjoyable. "So do not put me on the missing persons show."

Billy Weaver chuckled. "Man, you are something else. I can never tell if you're joking."

"I'm not. I will not be coming back." Frost glanced up. He liked Billy. The man was simple. He had a wife he loved, three daughters he bragged about whenever he had the chance, and hockey. "Thank you for letting me participate in your games."

"Wait, you can't just leave," Billy protested. "What's going on? Maybe the guys and I can help. Does this have anything to do with the fact you run off to the forest after the games? If you need a place to stay, someone will have a spare bedroom you can use. You don't have to squat in the forest. If you need money, I hear they're looking for help at the post office. Or, there are a couple of farms looking to hire handymen."

Frost began to speak, but one of the players skated close and yelled, "Blue!"

The call was answered as the others on the ice cried out, "Blue!"

Frost smiled and lifted his hand in greeting. It was then he noticed a woman watching the practice. She stood near the edge of the plastic barriers around the rink. A blue knitted cap held down her brown hair. Her dark coat was buttoned, the bulk of it, along with the bag she carried, hiding her shape. She held a device in front of her face, and his brain tried to connect the image with the right word. It did not seem to be in the language recognition uploads Galaxy Alien Mail Order Brides gave him.

"Her name is Meg Taylor," Billy said.

"What?" Frost looked at him in confusion.

The man laughed. "The woman you're staring at. Her name is Meg Taylor, and my wife tells me she's very single. She wants me to set her up with one of my friends. She used to be a big deal out in Chicago, but when her father became ill, she moved back to take care of him. I tell ya, she's a good one."

Meg lowered the device, and he was able to see her face. Some details were lost over the distance, but he found her exquisite. His eyes automatically dipped down to see her soft globes. They were hidden by her clothes.

"Does that stare mean we can count on you to stay?" Billy asked. "I can introduce you to Meg. It would make my wife happy."

"Yes," he whispered. Only to correct, "No. My family requires me to return. I'm sorry. I must go now. Thank you for your hospitality."

If he spoke to the woman, he might not be able to keep his promise to his brother. If he knew for sure it was fate that would be one thing. But the fact was, the quickening of his two hearts, the knots in his stomach, the pulsing vibration in his lower regions, they could be signs of desperation.

"I hear buzzing. I think your phone is going off," Billy said.

Frost didn't carry a phone.

He'd wanted this journey to work. He'd wished for it. He wanted a wife. He wanted love. That desire could fool him into believing in something that wasn't real. The idea that this woman, across a hockey rink, was meant for him went against all intergalactic odds.

"Goodbye, friend." Frost turned to leave and walked right into a metal trash bin. The rough edge tore his jeans and sliced open his leg.

"Oh, damn, you okay?" Billy tried to help Frost right himself.

"Yes."

It was a lie. He didn't feel okay. Earth, for all its people, felt like a lonely, lonely place. His eyes moved to where the woman watched him. He couldn't interact with any of them.

Stupid blue skin.

He wanted so badly to fit in, to belong, and that made him feel even more the outsider.

Frost ignored the pain in his leg as he hurried across the street. He would miss his new friends, but his love for his brothers was stronger. If there was a chance he had put them at risk, he had to rectify that.

The uneven sidewalk that cut through the small town led to a park that turned into woods. There he could walk the rest of the way back to Elle's home undetected. His feet sloshed in melted snow.

Frost kept his head down, hiding his face under the hood of his jacket. His thigh ached where it struck metal, but he ignored it. Cars passed, but he didn't look up. Tension rolled through him with the sound of each set of tires. He wasn't sure if he was being watched, or if it was just paranoia.

The park was empty, and he was able to quicken his pace. For a second, he tried to pretend the trees were poles of ice, but the brown color made it hard to imagine he was home.

The pain in his leg became more insistent. He glanced back to see drops of dark blue on the ground in a trail following him. There was no way he could heal with the warmth of the clothes on his body. He needed the cold. Unlike humans, low temperatures invigorated him.

Alone in the forest, he didn't think twice about disrobing as he tried to find a place to rest in the snow. He flicked the heels of his shoes with his toes to remove them without leaning over. He pulled off the jacket and shirt. Next, he unzipped the blue jeans and pushed them from his hips, careful not to further irritate the gash in his leg.

Frost didn't stop until he'd freed himself entirely of the alien clothing. Naked, he lay on the ground in a snow drift. He let the cold encase him as he sank into the snowy depths. The wound on his leg stopped throbbing and began to tingle. The blood inside him slowed and gave the injury time to heal itself.

"Meg Taylor." He said her name softly and let himself daydream. "Beautiful Meg Taylor."

5

MEG HAD TRIED TO TRAIL AFTER THE stranger and almost lost him when he cut through the park. At that point, she had to get out of her car and follow him on foot. The blue dye in the snow beside his tracks made him easy to trail.

The article had been right. There was a blue man on the hockey team they called Frost Chaos. She almost didn't believe it even as she'd looked through her viewfinder to take his picture. For some reason, she'd expected maybe a tribal face tattoo or streaks of body paint.

Meg wasn't in the habit of lying to herself and had to admit she felt something buzz through her the moment she zoomed in on him. The attraction was instant and unmistakable. He intrigued her.

There weren't many rebellious men in Rumble, and that flare of independence defined the type of man she always fell for. That strong attraction might have been what propelled her to go after him.

A small piece of her knew that following a stranger into the woods might not be the best idea, but the much larger journalistic part of her personality—the curious part that needed to ask questions and get answers—overruled it. Her father always said she'd been born with a significant awareness of the world around her, but sometimes lacked the common sense to stay out of it. Of course, he was usually referring to the times she did something dangerous or stupid—like trying to skateboard down a ramp to see if she could (she couldn't) or jumping into a lake on an old tire swing that happened to be home to a snake. The creature didn't like being swung, or wet, or her. It turned out that Joe Ingman had done it to scare her.

Her foot hit something hard, and it drew her from her thoughts. Meg looked down, finding a man's shoe. She picked it up. Still following the trail of blue droplets, she came upon a dark jacket like the one the man had worn, and then a shirt.

The fact that Frost might be naked caused her to walk faster.

This was odd. Who took their clothes off in winter? Well, besides those people who went skinny-dipping in frozen waters as part of a crazy people's polar club. Damn, that water had been unbearable, but she'd gotten her firsthand story.

Meg found his pants. The material was damp from the ground. She dropped the shoe and picked up the jeans. The same blue substance she'd found on the ground covered a jagged cut in the material. Touching it, she rubbed it between her fingers and then sniffed it. It had a musty scent, like autumn when the leaves were falling in the crisp air. It wasn't like any dye or paint she'd ever seen.

If the man's clothes were here, where was the man?

Meg followed the disturbed snow. It led to a large drift near a fallen log and what looked like the start of a snow angel without wings. A naked blue leg stood out in contrast to the white. He had sunk deep into the drift and wasn't moving.

She felt her entire body stiffen as she followed the leg with her eyes until it reached its natural conclusion—a blue penis sprinkled in white clumps of packed snow.

Every inch of the man was blue.

Every. Single. Freaking. Inch.

Her eyes darted to his face. His expression looked about as shocked as she felt. At least he was alive.

Meg glanced around before taking a step back. She realized the camera still hung around her neck and was tempted to take a picture she could study more in-depth later.

Frost rolled until he was sitting. His arms came forward to hide his male member.

How to explain her presence?

"You're blue," she said.

He merely stared up at her.

Oh, wow. That sounded professional.

Dumbass.

"I mean, are you all right? Your skin is blue. Do you need...?"

What? her inner voice mocked. *Do you need help for the hypothermia you are clearly not suffering from?*

"A, um..." She tried to force herself to sound thoughtful while not sneaking a peek at his blue penis.

Shit. Too late.

"Blanket? Do you need a blanket? Or help? Or, um...?"

Shit. Not again. Stop looking. Look at his face. His face. Face!

Wow. Those eyes are really ice blue.

There was no accounting for the hard jolt of arousal taking over her senses. Her body's needs warred with her head's logic until finally her brain decided to help fill in the fantasy. In no reality could she initiate the ideas streaming through her mind.

People said going without sex became easier in time.

People were wrong.

In the three years since she'd had sex, fantasies had become stockpiled in her daydreams. Frost ticked many of her erotic boxes—sexy naked stranger with an amazing body, alone in the wilderness with a hint of danger to get the heart-beat going; a rough, passionate claiming where he tore off her clothes and...

Meg glanced around, trying to see where they could go. The ground was too cold. Her car was too far away. Against a tree? Surely there would be a tree he could thrust her up against?

What the hell was she doing? None of that was going to happen. She couldn't fuck a stranger in the snow. That would be insane.

Oh, but she wanted to.

His jet-black hair fell against his cheeks and forehead, wet from the snow. Tattoos typically faded in spots and did not cover every single inch without some color variation. But if not a blue full-body tattoo, there had to be some kind of explanation. Though, one shoulder had darker blue markings that looked like a tribal design.

"Are you from Kentucky?" she asked.

"No, I am from this planet," he said. His voice caused a tiny shiver to work its way over her already amorous body.

Meg gave a small laugh at the joke. "I'm sorry, I know I was—*am*—staring. Forgive me for the rudeness. When I saw the clothes in the woods, and then you, I thought something had happened and you needed help, but evidently you're fine and..."

And I'm still staring at his snow-covered penis. Her inner voice sounded irritated.

"The blue mountain family in Kentucky had —*has?*—had a medical condition that made their skin, well, blue, and that's why I asked." Meg worked her fingers on her camera. She really wanted to snap a picture.

"There are blue people on Earth?" He rubbed his thigh around the same place she'd seen the tear in his jeans. A small dark line formed a scar there, but he did not appear freshly injured. The snow near his leg had more of the dark blue coloring.

Surely that wasn't blood? She glanced at her fingers where she'd touched it. The blue color stained the tips.

Her heartbeat quickened. Blue blood. Blue skin. Mentions of Earth rather than a particular country.

No. He couldn't be...

"You're right to mock me," Meg said. "I am out of practice. Please let me start over. My name is Meg Taylor, and I'm a writer. I saw the sports article about you in the paper and wanted to ask you a few questions."

"Because I am blue?" It didn't sound like a question.

She found no point in lying. "Partly, but also who you are and where you're from. Is your name really Frost Chaos? I can tell by your accent you might not be from America, or at least your family wasn't."

"You want to write about my blue and where I am from?" Frost stood.

Meg had not expected him to be so tall as he towered over her. She took an unconscious step back. The logical voice in her head yelled at her to run. The not-so-logical part stayed where she was, shaking legs and all.

"I'm sorry, but I cannot allow this," he said.

Frost didn't appear worried about the fact he stood naked in the snow. He showed no signs of being cold. Even with her layers, she felt the chill of approaching evening. Her breath came out in soft white puffs of air. His did not.

"Allow?" Meg repeated. She pushed the camera strap so it would hang over her back. He wouldn't be able to reach it if he tried. There was no way he was taking it from her. This was her story, and she would write it.

Hopefully.

Well, maybe, if she could get concrete facts.

Dammit, why wouldn't he answer her?

Tiny trails of water ran down his body as the snow melted on his shoulders, glistening in the sunlight like liquid diamonds. He did not appear to notice.

Meg was very aware of being alone with him.

The stillness of the forest was palpable. There was no breeze, no sound of wildlife. She'd been in the woods thousands of times, and they had never felt like this.

"You play hockey, which makes you a public figure in our small town of Rumble, and I'm a journalist." Her words were not as confident as she would have liked. "I can write about whatever I want."

"I no longer play hockey. So you will not write about me." Frost did not look away from her. His gaze penetrated.

"You quit the team? Why?" She tilted her head to the side, wishing she'd started the digital recorder on her phone, so she didn't forget anything. In Chicago, it was illegal to record a private conversation if all parties were not aware. However, she wasn't in Chicago anymore. Federal law and Minnesota law said it was all right to record as long as one person knew about it, even if that person was the one doing the recording.

Was it too late to reach for phone? Meg turned slightly and slid her hand into her messenger bag. Using her fingerprint to unlock the device, she glanced down and hit the recording app to turn it on. She held it up. "Do you mind if I use this to record what we talk about?"

He gave her a strange look. "I saw you at the rink. Why did you follow me?"

She debated a moment before turning the recorder off and dropped the phone back into her messenger bag. Her Chicago training made it hard to change her ways.

Muscles contracted as he stared at her like a wild animal ready to pounce. A low vibrating noise sounded. It came from his body, and she looked down to see his penis more clearly. Tiny bumps moved beneath the blue flesh and the noise pulsed in a steady rhythm.

That wasn't normal. It was sexy as sin, but not normal.

Meg looked at the imprint he'd left in the snow. If anyone else had lain like that, they'd be shivering and begging for a blanket.

Shit. What did I get myself into?

"I wanted..." Her breathing deepened, and her heartbeat quickened. Her foot crunched in the snow as she continued to back away. "I wanted to talk to you, but I can see you don't want to talk about...so I'll go."

"Do you hear that? Is someone else here?"

Frost frowned. "Did you bring someone with you?"

"What are you?" She searched his face. Every instinct she had screamed that this was more than a man who painted himself for the love of sports.

He did not look like he wanted to answer. "You will say nothing about—"

She yelped as he reached toward her. In her effort to get away, Meg tripped on something buried in the snow. Her limbs flailed, and she fell, not making good on her escape.

6

FROST STOOD OVER THE WOMAN LYING IN THE snow. Red colored the white from a wound on her head. His hand was still lifted toward her. He had wanted to catch her but looking at her had caused his body to vibrate, and his reactions had been too slow.

He'd chosen this part of the forest to heal for its privacy. As she'd stood over him, staring down, he'd been mesmerized and speechless. He hadn't been able to think of what to say. "I wish to mate with you" seemed a little too honest. "You make my body vibrate" was even more so.

"Meg?" Frost fell to his knees. He did not know how to help her. "Meg Taylor?"

The feeling of being watched didn't leave

him. Someone else was in the woods. He detected footsteps—one, two, pause, one, two, pause.

Frost scooped his arms beneath Meg's body and lifted her from the ground. Were all Earth women this light to carry? Her eyes didn't open.

One, two, pause, one, two, pause.

"Follow the..." a voice whispered.

He listened but could not make out any more words.

Frost didn't wait to see who was coming. He hated that Meg was injured but was glad for more time with her. There was something about her that mesmerized him. She jostled in his arms as he ran with her through the trees toward Elle's home. The urge to protect her was strong. Instinct told him the woods were not safe even if her body could have handled lying in the snow.

Elle's home was nestled in a clearing in the trees. It was the guesthouse of her parents' home, which stood several yards away. He did his best to stay out of view. The last thing he wanted was Elle's mother, Regina, to see him abducting a female while running naked in the woods. Regina already had a hard time accepting her daughter was with an extraterrestrial. Elle's father, Roger, on the other hand, might be slightly more understanding.

Slightly, but not much.

Frost carried the woman into the home and placed her on the couch. "Elle!"

Laughter came from a room at the end of the hall, and he rushed toward it. Without stopping to knock, he threw open the door. His brother was naked, standing by the bed, as his wife lay half exposed.

Elle gasped and covered her body.

"Frost," Ice warned.

"Elle, you must come. I think she's broken." Frost left the door open and went back to the living room.

Snow stood by the couch looking at Meg. "I don't remember this being here when I left this morning."

"Frost," Ice said, "my wife does not like it when you look at her naked. You can't—"

Elle pushed past Ice. She had pulled on jeans and a shirt. "You said *she*?"

Elle went to Meg, turning her head to the side to study the wound. "What happened?"

"Yeah, what did you do?" Snow asked. "I don't

think you're supposed to club the pretty ones over the head like that. It's bad for their brains."

"She fell." Frost ignored his brother.

"Where?" Elle continued to touch Meg, digging her fingers into the woman's hair.

"In the woods." Frost leaned over to see what Elle was looking at.

"Why were you naked in the woods?" Elle glanced at him with a strange expression on her face. "Never mind. I don't want to know."

"I cut my leg. I needed the cold to heal." Frost showed Elle his thigh, where a thin scar showed he'd healed. He then touched Meg's forehead. "Can you fix her?"

"She's not a car. She hit her head. We should get her to the hospital," Elle said.

"Did she see you like that?" Snow asked.

Frost nodded. "She followed me, and she wasn't the only one out there today. I heard foot-steps. I think I was being tracked."

"Tracked? Was it Milano's men?" Ice asked.

"I do not know. I didn't see them. I heard slow steps like when we track in the tundra and then whispering."

"It's probably hunters. It's deer season, and they're always wandering through this area, even though they shouldn't be. That's one of the reasons I keep telling you to be careful when you go out." Elle stood and went to a kitchen drawer, only to return with scissors. She cut the two straps off Meg's shoulder. "We need to make sure she doesn't have pictures. Here."

She handed the device and a bag to Ice, who in turn gave them to Frost. Elle went back to the kitchen.

Frost let the bag drop to the floor as he turned the other object in his hands. "What is it?"

"It's a camera. Did she aim it at you?" Elle wet a rag under the faucet and went back to Meg to dab at the head wound.

Frost realized what concerned Elle. "This weapon is not what hurt my leg. I scratched it on a trash bin."

Meg moaned.

Elle pointed at the weapon. "Hide that."

Snow picked up the bag from the floor and then grabbed the camera before disappearing up the stairs.

"Hey there, you're okay," Elle said softly. "You bumped your head."

Meg's lashes fluttered, and she looked up at Elle in confusion.

"Her name is Meg Taylor," Frost said.

Meg shifted her gaze from Elle to him. Seeing him, she gasped and sat up on the couch, pressing her back into it.

"Dammit, Frost, go put clothes on," Elle scolded. "Ice, you too. I've told you both you can't walk around here naked. It's not how we do things on this, um, in this...country."

"I have clothes, Elle," said Snow, who reappeared from upstairs, as if that made him the winner of a contest.

Frost stared at Meg. Her eyes focused on his face and she slowly felt her head.

"Frost—*oh my God.*" Elle stood in front of him and pushed his arm. "I did not need to see that. Get your vibrating ass upstairs now!"

"It's my penis, not my ass," Frost corrected.

Elle gave a dramatic shiver and closed her eyes. Without looking at him, she whispered, "Just go upstairs and find clothes. It will keep our guest from freaking out while I try to figure out how to explain...*everything*."

At that, he nodded and rushed to do as she ordered.

7

Meg didn't move as the man pressed his face close to hers. By his appearance, she could guess he was Frost's relative, except for one giant thing—his skin was a dark tan instead of blue.

"How's it going? Are you married?" the man asked, grinning. "I am looking to join with a mate as destined by the gods and you're pretty."

Meg kept her fingers pressed close to the throbbing wound on her head. The pressure helped ease the pain. "I...what?"

"You're pretty," the man repeated.

"What—huh?" She rubbed her fingers deeper.

"Snow, get out of that poor woman's face," the one they'd called Elle ordered before shoving the man back.

"I do not care if she does not have money," Snow said. "I can hunt."

Elle took a deep breath as if trying to muster patience. "Why don't you see if you can find where your brother left his clothes and bring them back?"

Snow grumbled but went to do as instructed. "Don't let Frost start any of the traditional fighting or hunting rituals until I have my fair chance to perform."

Meg glanced at her surroundings as she was left alone with Elle. The room looked like a normal living area in a well-kept house. Under most circumstances, it wouldn't be frightening. Considering Mr. Blue's brother wanted to have a ritual over her, the home felt a little too isolated in the woods. Horror movies started this way.

Though nice, nothing in the home indicated a family lived there. No portraits hung on the walls, only landscapes. No jackets were tossed over the backs of chairs, only folded throw blankets. The place looked more like a rental vacation home. It was too tidy, too neat, too impersonal.

"Hi...Meg, is it?" The woman knelt in front of her. She talked slowly and clearly. "My name is Elle. You fell and bumped your head. My friend brought you here so we could help you. Do you understand?"

Meg furrowed her brow and said wryly, "Thanks. My understanding of the English language is intact."

Elle sat back, surprised. "Oh, so you're not freaking out. That's great."

"Should I be freaking out? It's not like you're going to hold me prisoner." Meg arched a brow and waited for an answer. When it didn't come, she became a little worried. Maybe she should be freaking out right now. Her eyes went to the stairs. "Why is your friend...?"

"Blue?" Elle supplied.

"Naked in the middle of winter." Meg lifted to look out the window. She saw an expanse of snow and trees. Footsteps tracked through the yard as if it had been walked many times, or by many people.

"Everyone has their quirks," Elle dismissed.

"Where are we?" Meg eyed a dreamcatcher hanging on the wall. "I don't recognize the yard."

"I don't know why you would," Elle said.

"You look familiar." Meg tried to place where she'd seen the woman. "Are you from Rumble?"

"I went to school in Cedarmore," Elle said.

"Maybe that's where I've seen you. Our high school competitions." Meg tried to stand but felt dizzy. "How long was I out? Are we in Cedarmore?"

"You're someplace safe." Elle was clearly hiding something. She stood and didn't meet Meg's gaze. "Let me get you a clean rag."

Meg looked for anything that might tell her where she was. A piece of paper on the side table had strange symbols written on it.

"Is this some kind of club?" Meg stopped herself from saying cult. She reached for the scrap of paper and shoved it in her pocket while Elle was distracted. The fact that stealing was wrong caused her to second guess the action, but as Elle looked in her direction she couldn't bring herself to return the paper while the woman watched.

"No, we're a family." Elle returned and sat beside her on the couch. She tried to smile. Though her gestures were kind, there was a strange expression on the woman's face, almost as if she were afraid.

Meg's mind raced with questions. A cult family? Why did Frost's penis look like that? Body modification? Did he have tiny beads inserted beneath the skin? Why did the men talk like they just landed on the planet yesterday?

"It's genetic," Elle said, drawing Meg from her thoughts.

"What?"

"Frost's skin," Elle clarified. "It's a genetic condition."

"Like the blue Appalachian people who lived in the isolation of a hollow for so long that a family anomaly had turned a bunch of them blue," Meg said. It really was the only logical comparison she had.

"*O-kay*." Elle didn't sound convinced.

"You don't know what I'm talking about, do you?" Meg realized she still touched her head and lowered her hand to look at her blood-tinted fingers—one hand had blue, the other red.

Elle studied her. "What were you doing in the woods?"

"I was looking for an interview..." Meg glanced around. "My camera. Have you seen it?"

Elle shook her head in denial. "No, maybe Snow will find it in the woods."

Meg hoped so although the weather would not be good on the equipment.

"My husband and his brothers don't like to do

interviews," Elle said. "I'd appreciate it if you'd respect our privacy."

Meg would make no such promise. Her intuition was working overtime. There was more to this story than a blue man playing hockey. This family was hiding something bigger. She could feel it.

When Meg didn't speak, Elle asked, "How are you feeling? Do you want me to call an ambulance? You lost consciousness, but your pupils don't look dilated. Do you feel dizzy? Sick?"

"It's sore, and I have a little headache, but I think it's fine." She turned her hands to hide the bloody fingers. "I'd prefer if you didn't call an ambulance. I think they charge something in the way of five hundred dollars just to pick a person up, and I don't have an extra five of anything lying around."

"Maybe you should stay here for a while, just in case," Elle offered. "We could keep an eye on you and make sure you're not bleeding into your brain."

And I can figure out what the story is, Meg thought as she nodded in agreement.

Her father had Jenny Mirani to keep him company and would be fine. Meg usually left them alone on date nights, so he wouldn't be expecting her home for a while. If she was injured, the last thing he needed was for her to pass out on him and cause him to worry.

Even as she thought it she knew it was an excuse. She couldn't resist following a lead, and she couldn't resist finding out more about the sexy, mysterious Frost. Even though he was out of the room, the attraction she felt for him stayed strong.

"Milano!" Frost ran down the stairs, leaping over the last quarter to land on the floor. He wore jeans, a t-shirt, and sneakers.

Elle's pleasant demeanor instantly changed.

"What's Milano?" Meg asked.

They ignored her.

"Ice," Elle yelled as she ran to the counter to unplug a cellphone. "Grab the bag. We need to go. This is it!"

Ice appeared from a back room, also dressed. "How do you know?"

"Forest outside my window. Three that I could detect," Frost answered. "I'm sorry. I think they might have followed me from town."

"Isn't your brother in the forest right now?" Meg questioned. Again, they appeared to ignore her.

Elle dialed and then said into the phone, "It's happening. Keep away from the house for a few days and then report a break-in. You were boondocking in the RV, and you never saw us. I love you. I'll call as soon as I can."

"Where is Snow?" Frost asked.

Elle hung up. "I sent him to get your clothes. I want you two to take the car and meet me," she glanced at Meg, "at the place."

"I can't drive," Frost said.

"I think I can manage," Ice said.

Meg stiffened as all eyes turned toward her.

Ice's eyes narrowed. "We need a head start."

"I'm not stopping you," Meg answered.

Yet again, they ignored her.

"Do what you have to." Elle grabbed a knitted black hat and jacket from a coat closet. "We'll sort it out later. I'm going after Snow. I know the area. You two need to hide." She gave Ice a quick kiss. "Be safe."

"Protect yourself," Ice ordered.

Elle left her alone with the two men.

Ice pulled jackets out of the closet and threw one at Frost. "Get covered." He disappeared into the hallway.

"What's going on?" Meg demanded, her voice rising along with her panic. "What is Milano?"

"Bad humans who like to do bad things," Frost answered. "Come. We must go."

This had gone far enough. She needed to step back from the situation.

"I got it." Ice returned carrying a cloth bag.

"Elle should not be out on her own," Frost said. "This is my fault."

"I do not like it either, but my wife can take care of herself." When Ice looked at Meg, it was easy to see he did not think much of her. "And Elle won't be alone. I'm going after her. I didn't want to get into an argument, so I let her leave first."

"Then I am coming," Frost insisted.

"That is your responsibility." Ice pointed at Meg. He handed his brother the bag. "Take this. We'll follow behind in the car. If we don't arrive, you know what to do."

Ice disappeared down the hall, and she heard a back door opening.

"You can go with them. I'm fine here," Meg said.

"You must come with me." Frost waved his

hand as if he expected her to follow him down the hallway.

"No."

He came back into the living room. "Can you not walk?"

"No, I can walk fine. I'm just not leaving with you, crazy man." Meg gripped the couch. "You can go, but I'm not coming."

"You must," he insisted.

"No, I mustn't," she said.

He began walking away only to come back and gaze out the front window. She turned to see what he was looking at.

A hand clamped over her mouth, and an arm wrapped her waist like a vise. His skin was cold as he lifted her off the ground. Meg tried to scream as she kicked her legs and clawed his hand.

"Forgive my manhandling, but I am afraid you must."

8

Well, crap. He'd abducted a human.

This trip to Earth was not what Frost had planned, was not what he'd hoped for, and definitely was not what Galaxy Alien Mail Order Brides had promised him when he'd signed up to meet women. He had a few things he wanted to say to Bob and Gary when the ship landed.

Frost stared at Meg as she sat in the dirt against the wooden wall of the old barn. She touched her wounded head, but when he asked about it, she ignored his questions. In all honesty, he couldn't blame her. He had dragged her through the woods to an abandoned barn. Sintaz might lack in population and laws but taking people against their will was frowned upon in most galaxies.

He couldn't tell if Meg's expression was scared or angry, but her eyes followed his every movement. When he spoke, she refused to reply. It made apologizing difficult.

If he were truthful, he didn't know if he was scared or angry at the moment either.

Where were they? His family should have been there by now. Not knowing what was happening to them wasn't a pleasant feeling.

Frost paced the floor. Rusted pieces of metal littered the ground and hung from the rotted wood stalls. The sound of the wind whistled through cracks in the walls. "It should not be taking them this long."

Meg continued to stare at him. There was something about her face that made him ache deep inside. She was everything a man from another planet could want. Or, at least she could have been. He would never know her like he wanted to, but the idea of her would be his daydream on those long, cold days alone on Sintaz.

He had wanted so badly to find a place to fit in so he could stay on Earth, but it wasn't meant to be. "You should not have followed me from town. If I did not have to watch you, I could be helping my brothers."

"Don't blame me. I didn't make you kidnap me," Meg countered.

"You are correct. This is my fault. I went to town and tried to assimilate." Frost reached into the bag his brother had given him. The communication device was warm against his cooler hand. He had no choice but to call the Galaxy Brides ship back early. Nothing about this trip had gone as he'd hoped. He turned on the device but left it in the bag. "You should be safe in here."

He made his way toward the door.

"Wait," Meg ordered. She pushed up from the dirt floor. "You're just leaving me here?"

"Yes. I wish you a long and happy life." Frost strode from the barn. The evening was coming over the forest, and it brought with it a refreshing chill. He tried to hear movement in the trees as he willed Ice, Snow, and Elle to appear from within the woods.

"Seriously?" Meg demanded as she followed him out of the barn. "That's it?"

"Yes." Frost nodded at her once.

"Seriously?"

"Do you wish for me to say something else? I am sorry I have inconvenienced you. Goodbye, Meg." He headed up a small hill.

"Oh, no, you come back here. Why kidnap me in the first place if you're just going to make me sit in a dirty barn in the cold?" Meg followed him. "I think I deserve a real answer as to what is going on here."

"You are out of danger from Milano, and your wound appears manageable. There is no reason for me to keep you." He looked at the sky. The ship should be coming any time. At least, he hoped it would. Last time they'd called for help, Galaxy Brides hadn't been the most reliable of transports.

What would he do if Galaxy Brides abandoned them on Earth?

How would Frost find his brothers without their help? The planet was so big, and he didn't understand much of the alien society he now found himself in.

The fear of that thought gripped him so tightly he had to struggle to breathe. Frost's two hearts became erratic in their beats as if fighting each other for his life's fluid.

What if they left him, alone, on Earth, a blue freak being chased by mercenaries?

Meg grabbed him by the arm, shaking him from his spiraling thoughts. "Are you listening to me? I think I deserve some answers. What's going on here? Who are you?"

Frost pulled the communication beacon out of the bag and set it on the ground just in case the material blocked the signal. The blue light blinked steadily, calling for help. "You should hide in the barn until this is over. You will be safe there."

"Until what's over? Safe from what?" Meg reached for the beacon. "What is this thing?"

He grabbed her wrist and stopped her from picking up the device. "Do you really want answers? Because some things cannot be unlearned. It's not too late. You can still hide and pretend tonight never happened."

Frost felt the breeze shift. The color of the blinking light changed.

Thank the stars, the ship was coming.

Meg hesitated and then slowly nodded her head. "Yes, I'm sure I want to know. What is going on? Who are you?"

"Look up." Frost kept his voice soft. He

watched her confusion. She hesitated before doing as he requested.

Frost did not need to follow her gaze to know what she would see. Her expression changed with each passing second. First, the stars would disappear into blackness. Then, they would be replaced by a tiny hint of lights before finally the base of the ship would become unmistakable.

The wind picked up as the ship neared. Hair blew around Meg's head. Her eyes widened as her breath came in unsteady, shallow pants. She stood stiff, shaking as if she wanted to run but couldn't. Her fingers stretched wide, but she didn't reach for anything. "What? What? What?"

Frost touched her cheek, and the verbal panting stopped. She looked into his eyes. Warmth from her flesh tingled his fingers. The feeling worked its way down his body until he began to vibrate with need. Now was not the time for attraction.

"You're an extraterrestrial, an alien," she stated.

"Yes."

"And that's a spaceship." She looked up.

"Yes, it is."

"No." She shook her head in denial. "This

isn't real. Aliens aren't real. It's some kind of trick."

"You said you wanted to know. This is knowing." Frost wanted to be close to her. He wanted to freeze time. This moment would not last long. The spaceship would land. He would leave her to look for his brothers. After their last ordeal, Galaxy Brides claimed they wanted to make things right. This fleeting instant was all that was left of his freedom on Earth.

Frost leaned forward, pressing his mouth to hers. The shock of where his impulses led caused him to let go of her and step back. He lifted his hands as if to put a blockade between them. "I don't know why I did that."

Meg appeared torn between looking at him and staring at the ship. He imagined she could not process what was happening. He'd been a young boy when he saw his first ship land, but he'd known about life on other planets when it arrived.

"Am I being abducted by aliens?" she asked.

Frost finally glanced up. The spaceship was landing a little too close to where they stood. He grabbed her by the arm and pulled, forcing her to stumble down the hill. She didn't protest as she kept her eyes on the craft.

When he deemed they were at a safe enough distance, he let go. She still stared at the landing ship.

"This isn't real," she whispered.

"Yes, it is."

"But your brothers aren't blue," Meg said. "And Elle looks human."

"Elle is human," Frost answered. "My brothers have altered their skin to blend in."

"That seems..." Her words were stunted. "It seems wrong to hide like that."

"Do you think humans would accept us if they knew who we really were?" Frost asked, trying not to sound too hopeful.

"No." Meg shook her head. The gust of air coming from the ship became stronger. Her hand reached absently towards him, the fingers clutching at air. "They would lock you up out of fear and do weird experiments on you." She turned to him when he didn't touch her and dropped her hand. "That's what you're afraid of, isn't it? Is that what Milano means?"

"The Milano Foundation took my brother when we first landed. He barely escaped, and then only thanks to Elle, who betrayed the company she worked for to do it. We thought we were safe here, but I ruined it by playing hockey."

The ship creaked as it touched down and the wind stopped with a final crescendo of leaves swaying in the trees.

Meg frowned. "You mean that thing wannabe-celebrity Franky 'The Heart Attack' Milano is always bragging about on television? I thought they were a charity feeding kids or something. What did they want with your brother?"

"Just as you suspected. They wanted to experiment. They took his fluids and locked him in a cage. They beat him, starved him, taunted him." Frost frowned to know that the organization could again be doing that very same thing. "It was a mistake for us to stay. We should have left when we had the chance. Maybe we can find another planet where Elle will survive, and we can all live. I don't know where that might be, but I do know Milano will not give us peace."

"Then why did you stay?"

Frost didn't answer. The sound of sliding metal drew her attention, and she moved closer to him. She held on to his arm with shaking hands, leaning behind him as if he could shield her.

Frost pulled his arm free from her grip and wrapped it around her. He drew her to his chest.

The protective gesture was a mistake. It brought her body too close to his, causing his vibrations to become even more intense.

Bob and Gary appeared in the entryway of the ship. They had donned skin suits as a disguise, which looked ridiculous as the material pulled tightly over their frames. They were short, stocky creatures with heads that were too big to be mistaken for human. Their shiny black hair was the same length all the way around their heads and was as fake as the rest of their outfits.

"Please don't let them hurt me," Meg said.

Frost tightened his grip. The only way Gary and Bob could hurt anyone was with their incompetence. So, yeah, there was a real danger there.

"Greetings, Frost," Bob said, using the Earth language. He'd tried to learn to speak Sintazian, but his grasp of the nuances had been worse than the translators. "I see you have found a bride. Welcome, human, please board and we will take you to your new home. Did you bring luggage?"

Meg gasped and pushed against his chest. He let her go, and she stepped away from him, putting distance between herself and the alien visitors.

"You have caused her to panic, Bob." Gary lifted a device and pointed it at Meg.

She screamed and began to run. Frost tried to stop him, but Gary managed to get a blast off before he could jump in front of him.

The screaming stopped, and Meg crumpled on the ground into the snow.

"There we go," Gary said.

"What did you do?" Frost demanded, even as he knew the answer. She would not be waking up for a while. He hurried to her and lifted her from the ground to cradle her in his arms. It was not lost on him that this was the second time that day he had carried her unconscious body.

"Sadly, these Earthlings are a timid lot. She is not the first bride who's tried to run at the sight of a spaceship," Gary answered. "Human women are especially delicate in temperament. It is one of the reasons we cannot transport them to other planets before they are chosen as mates." He put his blaster back into the holster and patted it a few times. "We always come prepared."

"She's not my bride," Frost said.

"Oh?" Gary shared what could have been a disappointed look with his partner.

Bob shook his head. "As per the agreement

you signed with Galaxy Alien Mail Order Brides, we cannot officially support the taking of non-marriageable Earth women from the bridal stock planet. At this time, only those who have mated can be given transport." He gave a stunted laugh. "It is not like we are Kintoks."

Gary's strange laughter joined Bob's. Kintoks were known sex traders. Frost was not amused.

Bob made a clicking sound before he continued, "We found we had to clarify this point after a failed trip to Las Vegas. Some of the grooms tried to bring women onboard in suitcases. They were unsuccessful, but we had much to answer for. It is also why we are taking smaller groups on these trips."

"I thought that was because people didn't trust the company after we lost—" Gary inserted.

"We misplaced a few Killians for a tiny amount of time." Bob shook his hands as if it was of no concern.

"Like you misplaced Ice?" Frost insisted. "Because—"

"Regulations have since been tightened for the safety of all," Bob interrupted. "The policy is very clear on this point. I realize Earth has many women, and in variety, but you are only allowed one—"

"Well, two in some cultural situations," Gary inserted.

"You are only allowed two," Bob corrected, "but both must be mated in accordance with—"

"Would you stop talking?" Frost carried Meg up the hill and walked past the aliens toward the ship's opening. "I don't care what your regulations say. My family is in danger, and you're going to help me rescue them."

"What have they done?" Bob didn't sound too worried. "Is it a matter of local law enforcement? We can easily clear up those concerns."

"Was it ice cream? That substance has been known to—" Gary started to say.

"Again, that's Killians," Bob cut him off. "Ice cream addiction is a serious problem, but not one we concern ourselves with for Sintazians."

"Whatever you said you were doing to keep us safe didn't work. Milano found us. I brought Meg to safety while Elle and Ice went to help Snow." Frost tried to step onto the ship, but an invisible barrier thrust him back. He managed to hold on to Elle as he regained his footing.

"Leave the non-mate on the ground. She'll be

fine. We will go now to look for your brothers." Bob scurried past him, pointing a device at the door so he could go through.

"I'm not leaving her on the ground in the wild." He again tried to carry her onboard, and he was again bounced back.

"Scans of this area show the only potential danger is a colony of humans," Gary said. "Since she is one of them, she should be unharmed."

"Fine. I chose this one. Meg's my mate. She loves me," Frost lied. "I wanted my brothers to be the first to know."

"Oh, well, that changes everything. Another happy union of joined hearts," Gary announced. "We have nearly a perfect record," his voice lowered, "for this flight," before rising again. "This is why we do what we do."

"My family," Frost insisted. This time, he tested the barrier with his toe instead of walking into an invisible wall. It finally let him pass. He carried Meg into the spaceship. Bob had disappeared.

"The Milano Foundation is a much bigger network than we anticipated. We have leaked the location of the desert facility where they held Ice to the authorities and news outlets without telling the nature of his origins, and we are in the process of tracking their leaders," Gary said.

"And you think that will stop them?" Frost wasn't sure it would matter.

"We have done extensive research on Earth culture. We believe we can manipulate their news for our purposes." Gary nodded.

"It obviously wasn't good enough. They still have my family. That is the only reason I can think of that they did not meet where we prearranged."

"We are tracking your brothers now," Gary assured him. "All will be well. Dr. Hanklen has been particularly difficult to find, but we have a location on Dr. Petals and hope she will lead us to him. If we stop Hanklen and Milano, the network should fall apart."

"How are you tracking them?" Frost frowned. "I didn't tell you where I'd last seen them."

"After Ice's unfortunate run-in with Earth factions, we decided it would be best if we used more archaic means of tracking you and your brothers during your stay."

"Meaning?" Frost went to put Meg in a seat and strapped her in, so she wouldn't become injured in flight.

"We placed locator chips inside you." Gary gestured toward Frost's hip.

"When? We didn't consent to that." Frost frowned. These two idiots better be tracking his brothers and not a couple of rogue Killians or whoever else they'd lost on this planet.

"Yes. You said, do whatever you must to keep us safe," Gary reminded him. "It was during that unpleasantness when you had me tied to a chair. I thought about melting the ties, but you seemed comforted by the idea that I was your prisoner and we are tasked with making your trip as comfortable as possible." Gary frowned. "You're not thinking of doing that again, are you? New regulations state that I'm not allowed to play hostage to hosted aliens."

Frost touched Meg's cheek, hoping that he had her adjusted in a comfortable position. "We should never have come to this planet."

"But this trip is a great success," Gary exclaimed. "Two of you have mated. It will inspire many more to sign on for marital trips."

"You should find a better planet. Earth does not want aliens coming here for women." Frost felt the spacecraft rock as the engine engaged. "We should have left when we found Ice the first time. I was blinded by hope after seeing him with Elle."

"And look how well it's turned out." Gary tugged at his skinsuit to adjust the face.

"My brothers and new sister are missing, presumably to be tortured by Earth psychopaths. I don't know how you can keep calling that a success."

"Strap in," Gary ordered. "We can't stay on the ground too long."

Frost took the seat next to Meg. He wasn't letting her out of his sight.

"I think I know what is happening. We are prepared for this discussion. You are worried about performing the coupling part of the mating ritual." Gary strapped in next to him. Frost wished he hadn't sat so close. The temptation to thrust the heel of his hand into the alien's jaw was overwhelming.

"No. I am worried about my family," Frost corrected.

"The urges in your body are natural," Gary assured him. "You should expect the human to accept you through an opening in her stomach about once a star cycle. When the female is ready, the teeth will retract into the skin to allow for this."

Frost flinched and looked at Meg's stomach. He'd seen Earth sex shows. Elle said it was called cable TV. He was pretty sure that's not what happened.

"If you have questions, I'll be happy to explain in more detail," Gary said.

"Stop talking," Frost ordered. "Concentrate on locating my brothers."

"Have you ever thought about being on a holobox? We'd love to include your testimonial about how happy you are to have met Legs. Any chance you will produce offspring soon? We could use—"

"Her name is Meg."

"Yes, Meg. A strange, but fine name." Gary patted his leg. "Don't worry. Maybe we can find her a new one before we take you back to Sintaz."

Frost's fingers tensed and stretched. Just one hit. That is all he wanted. It might be a mistake, but it would almost be worth it.

9

MEG COULDN'T MOVE. SHE FELT WEIGHED down. No not weighed, tied. She was tied down.

Remembering the landing spaceship and terrifyingly bad costumed aliens, she began struggling violently against her restraints. She jerked every part of her body she could get to move, trying to break free. She screamed, even before her eyes opened.

"You are safe." A voice tried to penetrate her frantic thoughts. Meg felt a cool hand on her arm and tensed. She breathed heavily.

Her eyes darted around, trying to focus but unable to stop on any one object long enough to figure out what was happening. The metal room had round lights, and grates, and protrusions.

What she took to be paint shimmered and changed like an electronic billboard. None of the languages looked familiar, even the lettering didn't appear to be human except for some Egyptian hieroglyphs. Finally, English appeared, and she read, "Welcome to Galaxy Alien Mail Order Brides, where we are joining hearts across the universes."

Aliens. Brides. Abduction. Blue. Frost. Spaceship.

Her thoughts were a stream of random words as she tried to construct a coherent notion of what was happening. Her body tingled, especially her back. She vaguely remembered hearing a blast before nothing. Had they shot her?

Spaceship abduction.

No, this couldn't be happening. She needed to get home to her father.

Her entire body shook violently.

"I'm going to unstrap your head." Frost leaned forward, coming into her view. She heard metal clang and felt her weight shift in the seat as the ship moved. He unstrapped her head and then loosened the ties holding her arms and chest.

"Where?" she managed, the sound barely

making it out of her mouth. "Who? What? Where?"

"I'm Frost. Don't you remember me?"

"He's your husband," another voice added. She couldn't see the bearer. "Congratulations!"

Meg's throat tightened, and she squeaked instead of talked.

"We were just discussing how long it will be until you have offspring," the voice continued.

"Don't listen to him." Frost kept his face in front of hers, blocking her view. "We're not married, and I'm not trying to impregnate you."

Those words should have caused her some relief. Instead, Meg was almost disappointed. She blinked hard, trying to focus her vision so she could better study his face. Ice-blue eyes met hers. The skin tone didn't bother her. She supposed it should have, but it didn't.

"I don't care that you're blue," she said softly.

"I don't care that you're not blue," he answered.

"I didn't mean for you two to make the baby now, in front of me. Don't worry. I won't peek. Go ahead," the other voice said.

"Shut up, Bob," Frost ordered.

"I'm Gary."

"Shut up, Gary," Meg said, not taking her eyes from Frost's.

His expression calmed her, and as she regained some of her faculties, she was able to force herself to concentrate on facts.

Fact one: her father was right, she leapt before thinking way too often.

Fact two: she was on a spaceship with aliens.

Fact three: she was sexually attracted to a blue man who liked hockey and came from...

"Where did you say you are from?" she asked.

"Sintaz," he answered.

Fact three: she wanted to kiss a blue man from Sintaz.

Fact four: she was going to kiss a blue man from Sintaz.

Meg felt the cool press of lips to hers before she realized what she had done. She remembered him kissing her on the ground before the ship landed and, now, staring into his gaze, she wanted to continue that experience.

Her heart beat faster, and she felt the spacecraft vibrate as it moved. The smell of autumn leaves became strong, reminding her of pumpkin pie and ridiculous table decorations made out of gourds. She lifted her arm, forcing the loosened strap against her chest to slide up. His skin was chilly. It was a strange sensation.

She was a writer. She could do better than strange—peculiar, bizarre, weird, extraordinary, unexpected, sensational. His tongue touched hers, and she gasped as a direct wave of desire made its way down her tingling, vibrating body to her sex.

Oh, fuck, pleasurable. The word is pleasurable.

She squirmed in the hard seat. The mindless pleasure caused her thighs to open and close. She wanted to claw her way free and throw him on the ground like a wild animal in heat.

"Don't be afraid of the stomach teeth," Gary whispered, none too softly.

The sound of the other man's voice hit her shaking body like a bed of spikes—unwelcome and highly disagreeable.

Meg tried to control her panting breath as she broke the kiss. She realized her hand was balled into his jacket, forcing him to her. The pulsations came from his body, not the ship. She remembered seeing his vibrating penis when he stood naked in the snow. The alien was a walking vibrator. That knowledge did not help to calm the ache in her sex.

Several more metal clanks banged around the

ship. Frost furrowed his brow, pulling away from her to reveal the bearer of the voice. The large-headed man with stretched skin was not what she'd expected. His shiny black hair looked like cheap polyester from a Halloween costume. If she hadn't seen the ship land for herself, she would have thought this was a prank.

"Hi. I'm Gary," the alien said. "You are going to love Sintaz. It's, um, cold."

Meg shook her head, the motion jerky as she tried to speak. "I can't leave my father. He's..."

"Parental figures?" Gary gave a strange click, and he unbuckled himself and stood. "I will have to ask about extended family passengers. No one has ever tried to bring their father as part of the bridal arrangement."

Meg waited until the strange alien made his way through a sliding metal door before saying to Frost, "My father needs me. I can't leave him. He is all I have."

Frost nodded. "I understand. Family is important. Ignore Gary. We are not abducting you. I have learned Earth women don't wish to be stolen."

"You learned?" Meg would have laughed if she wasn't still processing her situation. As it was, her emotions ran from panic to curiosity to terror to irrational.

"Yes. Elle taught us that Earth women like to be coaxed, but not abducted." Frost leaned forward to whisper, "I think she likes to do the abducting. When we landed, she captured my brother and put him in a cage. But then she saved him."

"Oh, ah, okay?"

"Would you like to put me in a cage, Meg?" he asked.

Her body still hummed with awareness. There were a lot of things she wanted to do to him. Putting him in a cage was not one of them. "No. The only people who belong in cages are those who pose a danger to society."

Was that disappointment in his expression? She wasn't sure.

"On Sintaz, we lock those people in an ice cave until we can transport them off planet. There are not many people left on my home world."

Meg started to nod only to laugh. "Wait. Are you saying that nearly everyone posed a threat to society, and you shipped them off?"

"No. People left because living on Sintaz is difficult. They'd rather work in cold storage on cargo ships. Some even hitched rides with the ESC."

"ESC?"

"Exploratory Science Commission," he explained. "They travel to many planets in search—"

"Many," she took a deep breath, "planets."

He nodded.

"How many planets?"

"I am not sure. I have not seen their flight records."

Meg closed her eyes and shook her head. "I mean how many alien planets are out there? Two? Three? A billion?"

"I do not know. Thousands? I have not thought to inquire." Frost slipped his hand onto her knee. "I would enjoy continuing to speak to you, but I must see what is happening with my family."

Meg nodded. "I understand."

He unbuckled his belt.

She reached to feel along her shoulder, also wanting to be free. Before he could go, she said, "Please don't leave me here."

Frost nodded and freed her from the seat. When she tried to stand, her legs were shaking so badly that she swayed. Frost caught her around the waist and held her upright. Even with his jacket, he felt cold.

"Are you always this temperature?" She slid her fingers over his exposed neck.

"Only when it is too warm," he said. "When it is colder, I am warmer. When it is warmer, I am colder. Does it make you uncomfortable?"

What made her uncomfortable was the need still centered low in her belly. Being close to his vibrating manhood didn't help. Her fingers worked against his skin.

A strong heartbeat thumped against where her arm touched his chest. The beat was not like a human's. His ice-blue eyes seemed to glaze over as he closed them.

"I am told there is a moist place between your thighs where I may place myself." Frost's bold words were so earnest that she had to keep from laughing out of shock. "I have wanted to vibrate within you from the first moment I saw you with your weapon device at the ice rink. We are compatible humanoids if that is a concern."

Tell him no, her mind pleaded. *You know this won't work, Meg. You can't fuck an alien. Who knows what diseases or pregnancies or...*

He shifted his hips, and his vibrating penis hit her stomach.

...or how good it will feel, her body seemed to answer. *No one will know. Can you really pass up such an experience? How can you call yourself a reporter if you don't jump in full force and experience?*

Her body had a fair point.

"Will you let me feel it?" he asked. "My brother has explained what to do. He has sex with his wife, Elle."

How in the world did she answer that?

"He said that Earth humans prefer to bounce apart and together, rather than join and vibrate. I find this strange, but he assured me that Earthlings have found a much better way to join and that I should let—"

Meg placed her hand on his mouth to stop his talking. There was only so much strange a woman could process in one sitting.

Meg looked around the metal room, seeing more of it now she was out of the chair. They were the only two there. Rows of empty chairs filled the area, configured in circular patterns. Not all of them were shaped to hold humanoids. Some of the seats were long and narrow. Others had enough molded indentations to fit a three-ass-cheeked alien. Then there were some that seemed to be a combination of both—three ass cheeks and a very long center protrusion in the middle that looked speciously like a dick and balls.

"You are trembling," Frost said. He started to let go of her, but she grabbed his jacket.

"Can I be honest?"

"I feel that is usually best."

"My brain can't decide if I'm fascinated, terrified, or sexually aroused. I want to scream. I want to ask questions. I want to kiss you." Meg shivered. She looked along the ceiling. Strips of lights ran over the metal in pulsating colors. "Can anyone hear or see us in here?"

"We are the only two in this room," he replied, stating the obvious. Again, he looked earnest, so it was hard to take his words for rudeness.

"I meant cameras or intercoms or something," she clarified. "Are we being watched? I don't want to end up in some kind of alien reality television show."

"I do not believe anyone is watching us."

"All right, then let's do this." Meg lifted on her toes and wrapped her arms around his neck.

Taken by an alien in a spaceship. Why not?

I'm fucking insane.

Am I really doing this?

Okay, then.

She hesitated before kissing him.

Frost reminded her of the days leading up to winter. The smell of autumn leaves falling in the crisp morning air, musty and fresh at the same time. Every inch of her tingled as the vibrations grew. They tickled her nipples through her clothes and teased her already sensitive sex.

Their mouths moved as if to test the other's responses. She suddenly realized that, for as strange as this was for her, it had to be just as odd for him. As far as the rest of the universe was concerned, she was as much an alien as he was. A cool tongue ran alongside hers. He tasted like a spice cake—not strong or unpleasantly so, but a hint of flavor that made her want to devour his mouth with hers.

Frost broke the kiss first, and she tried to follow his lips with hers to bring him back. "I wish to disrobe you."

Meg nodded. The tiny voice of reason she rarely listened to screamed at her to consider her actions. She found no reason to heed its practical advice, not when Frost made her feel so good.

The idea that someone (some *alien*) might walk in on them caused a small tremor to work through her. For that reason, she left her t-shirt on. Meg kicked off her boots and unbuttoned her blue jeans. She slid them down her hips, along with her panties to expose her legs.

Frost fumbled with his jeans but managed to push them off his hips before shrugging out of his jacket. He kicked his shoes from his feet and stepped out of the discarded jeans. His eyes watched her intently, focusing mostly on her thighs. He pulled the t-shirt from his chest and stood naked. The dark blue marks on one arm etched a pattern over his biceps to his chest.

Aside from the skin color, he looked human. Her eyes went to his cock. Well, *humanoid*, at least.

His shaft was erect, long, and thicker at the base than the tip. Tiny bumps moved beneath the skin, provoking her already heated body as they vibrated with sensual promise. The vibrations came in pulsing waves of sound.

Frost reached for her shirt, lifting it to expose her stomach and chest. He appeared deep in thought as he touched a breast to make it jiggle.

His fingers spread, and he grabbed hold and shook. "Fascinating."

Frost then pushed his fingertip into her belly button. Meg jumped in surprise.

"Does it open?" He tried to push it again.

Meg's muscles tensed in reflex as she leaned away from his finger. Then, grabbing his hand, she drew it between her legs. "No, but this will."

Frost pushed his fingers up. The movement put pressure on her clit as one finger glided into her. He wiggled it around to test the area. A second finger joined the first. She gasped as he slid them deeper.

Frost smiled and nodded. His fingers moved more insistently. "I do not feel teeth. This wetness will do nicely."

"I don't know where that came from, but Earth women generally don't have teeth down there." Meg reached for his cock. It only seemed fair she test it as he tested her. The vibrating bumps moved beneath her hand, firm, even as they become engorged. The man was a walking vibrator.

"How do I make your hole vibrate?" he asked, still exploring.

"I don't vibrate like you." Her words were panted.

"Then how do I know when it is ready to be entered?"

Meg knew that question deserved a long answer, but she didn't want to waste time explaining. "When my pussy is wet, it is ready."

Frost pulled his fingers out, and she missed the pressure inside her. Meg glanced around, looking for a place to shove him down so she could ride him. He lifted his fingers and licked. "It is ready."

Before she could answer, he spun her around and pushed her forward. She grabbed a chair for support and stood with her ass in the air. Frost came up behind her. Being out of the warm clothes had caused his temperature to rise, and his chilly body had warmed. His fingers probed her again, slipping until he found entry. Then, he drew his cock to her and thrust the full length of it in.

Meg had been without sex for a while, and the tight fit combined with the vibrations made her jerk violently.

Frost instantly pulled out and released her.

He said something in a guttural alien language before adding, "Did I injure you?"

Meg moaned and shook her head in denial as she faced him. Taking his hand, she led him toward one of the larger alien chairs and made him sit down before straddling him. She positioned her body to take him once more and lowered herself onto his shaft.

Her eyes met his—and at that moment, she didn't care about blue skin, or spaceships, or alien life. There was a connection, an invisible line that pulled them together. It locked their gazes as well as their bodies.

The vibrating bumps hit all the right places. Never had a man brought her so close to orgasming so quickly. She rocked against him, riding the pleasure he gave her. The heat between them built as it seemed to flood his body.

Meg came. Hard. The climax did not stop his penis from vibrating. If anything, it became more forceful.

"It is soft inside you," he said, still rocking even as she was nearly spent.

Suddenly, he took hold of her hips and held her tight to him. His shaft pulsed inside and what felt like an electric shock zapped through her. She felt him in that transference of energy. Every inch of her tingled in appreciation, and an intense heat washed over her, flushing her skin.

"What was that?" Meg whispered. She stretched and closed her fingers, feeling as if a magical current would shoot from the tips at any second.

"That, my beautiful human, was perfection. Ice was right. Earth sex is much better than Sintazian ways."

10

Frost was in love.

It had to be love. How else could he feel like this?

It wasn't just the sex though that had been wonderful. What he had inside him was a feeling, an instinct. Meg was everything he'd ever wanted —brave, smart, beautiful.

He watched her bend over to retrieve her clothing and instantly wanted to have Earth sex with her again. Sintazians merely joined, held still, and vibrated. Movement was definitely more fun.

Meg caught him staring and gave him a small smile. Her lips parted as if she would speak, but the door slid open. Her eyes rounded, and she scrambled to hide behind the chairs with her pants and a shoe.

Gary rushed inside. "We have located the trackers. Ice and Snow are together moving down *—oh, you're procreating!* Please, by all means, carry on. I can wait."

"My family cannot wait." Frost pulled on his jeans but didn't bother with a shirt. Guilt filled him at having succumbed to his base desires while his family was in trouble. He could not lose sight of what mattered. "Where are they?"

"Either running extremely fast or in a vehicle," Gary answered.

"A vehicle going where?" Frost prompted.

"South down the planet's surface." Gary leaned as if trying to see Meg. Frost stepped in front of him to block his view.

"How are you going to stop it?" Meg appeared from her hiding place. Her clothes were disheveled, but on. She wore one shoe and went to gather the other one. "Can you transport them out of there?"

Gary clicked a few times.

"What do you mean?" Frost asked.

"Beam them up, teleport them, move their matter from one place to another," Meg said.

Gary clicked faster. Frost realized it was some kind of laughter. "Sintazians cannot teleport. You are thinking of the Portare people."

"Take us to a viewing screen," Frost ordered. He motioned his hand that Meg should come with them. She shoved her foot into her shoe and bounced a few times before rushing to his side. Her hand glided up the back of his arm. Gary led them from the room, rambling about how a Portare once appeared in his food preparation area.

"Are you...?" Frost kept his voice low, even as he wasn't sure what he was asking Meg.

"I am," she nodded and squeezed his naked biceps tighter. It was pleasant not having to wear a shirt and jacket. He felt as if he could breathe easier.

"You might find this interesting." Gary reached out his hand and slid it along the wall. A viewing portal opened to show outer space.

Meg gasped and gripped his arm before slowly letting go. She reached forward as she stepped. Her fingers touched the portal. Her home world appeared to glow against the deep black of space. "I never in a million years thought I would see this."

"Your planet is very colorful," he said.

"Sintaz doesn't look like this?" Meg questioned.

"That floating ice ball?" Gary blurted before quickly amending, "Is very lovely."

Frost ignored the annoying alien. "My home world is very white with hints of blue. Much like your Arctic areas."

"No wonder you're adapted to the cold. Not many humans venture toward the poles." Meg ran her fingers in a circle, outlining Earth.

"I do not blame humans for staying away from that territory," Frost said. "I would not wish to disturb the cookie monster's lair. It would be frightening enough to have to leave offerings, knowing he attacks houses once a year looking to kidnap more pointy-eared children for his factories."

Meg gave him a strange look. "Are you talking about Santa Claus?"

Frost put a hand on her arm. "I hope your people are someday able to stop his reign of terror."

"Uh..." She appeared at a loss for words. Apparently, the very thought of this monster terrified the speech from her. Perhaps this was too painful a subject for her to talk about.

"You may stay and look, but I must go to my brothers." He did not want to rush her.

"No, I'll come with you." Meg looked expectantly at Gary. "His brothers?"

"Yes, yes, of course, this way." Gary continued down the ship's corridor of grated floors and metal walls illuminated by strips of light.

Gary led them through a series of sliding doors before finally reaching a cockpit.

Bob sat with his feet pressed against a wall slurping a yellow sludge from a bowl. Seeing them, he spastically jerked as he tried to right himself and hide the food. "What do we have here? Visitors?" He narrowed his eyes at Gary and did not seem pleased. "In the cockpit?"

"Where are my brothers?" Frost demanded. He looked at the numerous buttons, trying to find one that would show him what he wanted.

"I'm tracking them." Bob pointed at a panel next to his chair. The ghost of an image filled the screen—the tops of trees and the convoy of trucks moving through them. "Those two blue dashes are your brothers. The yellow are humans."

"There is a yellow by the blue. Maybe that's Elle," Meg said. "At least we know they're alive."

That didn't make him feel better. They may be alive, but what was the Milano Foundation doing to them? Ice's description of his treatment had been horrific. They beat him, experimented on him, and starved him. The torture had been getting progressively worse and, if not for Elle saving him, Ice was convinced he would be dead by now.

"Take me down there," Frost commanded. "I must free them."

"It is daylight now. It will be best to land the ship while it is dark if we are going close to Milano's mercenaries." Bob pointed to the convoy. "If they stay on this route, we should be able to reach them along this area of dense forestry by nightfall. If we try to extract them from their captors, it will be there."

"We're in a spaceship, and they're on the move." Meg leaned over the panel, studying the images. "If we attack, we don't know what they will do. We have to make a plan, so they don't hurt their prisoners."

"We?" Frost studied her face. Was she saying she wanted to be with him?

"This is going to sound lame, but what if we block the road somehow and stop them? They're in the last truck. Maybe then we can sneak up behind," she pointed at the blue slashes, "and get them out without being noticed."

"That is too dangerous for you," Frost dismissed. "However, it is a good plan. I will go."

"Want us to come?" Bob asked.

"No. I'll need you to do something to get those trucks to stop." Frost absolutely did not want Bob and Gary fucking things up for him. "I will take whatever weapons you have."

"How can I help?" Meg asked.

Frost looked at her beautiful face. Her body was fragile and not made for combat. "When we land, I want you to get off this ship and run for safety. You're human. You will find other humans to help you get home."

"I..." She took a deep breath and nodded. "Yes. I can do that. I know when I'm out of my depth. But when it's done, you'll let me know you're okay, won't you?"

"Gary and Bob will make sure you receive word of what happens." Frost pulled her against his chest and held her, knowing this might be the last time they were together. If he weren't killed trying to rescue his family, then he'd most likely be on a one-way trip off Earth. It was a trip Meg could not take. Her delicate body would not survive on Sintaz, and she had her own family responsibilities to see to.

Yes. This feeling had to be love. Nothing else would hurt this badly.

11

AS HE RAN THROUGH THE FOREST, HE PRAYED Meg found safety. He'd asked Gary and Bob to track her to make sure. Meg's last kiss lingered on his lips, a bittersweet reminder of all he couldn't have on Earth.

The air was cool but not as cold as he would have liked. At least there were patches of snow on the ground in case his brothers were injured.

He slowed to listen as he heard truck engines in the distance before speeding up his pace once more. Trees lined the road, giving him plenty of cover as he ducked behind saplings and underbrush.

Headlights appeared out of the darkness, charging down the road like the eyes of an angry beast. The sound of the engine drowned out any hint of wildlife. A small cargo truck passed, its size unimpressive compared to the sound it made. From the scan he'd seen on the Galaxy Brides ship, he knew there to be approximately five people inside. The second vehicle, a pickup truck, had only a driver. The third, a semi hauling a short trailer, carried Ice, Snow, and four others.

His eyes focused on the last vehicle.

Where were Bob and Gary with the distraction?

The vehicles rolled past, not stopping.

He cursed as he jumped out from hiding and ran after the tail lights.

Suddenly, brakes squealed, and tires slid. One of the vehicles struck another with a loud *bang!* The last vehicle skidded to a stop, and the semi's trailer jackknifed to the left.

Frost leapt back into the trees alongside the road, trying to see what was happening. He'd expected a fallen log or some kind of debris blocking the path. Instead, a row of familiar women stood in the way. It took him a moment to place them, but he finally realized they were from the holobox advertisement Bob had given him when they'd first met—options one through five.

"Hello boys," the Earth woman in a sparkling gown with blonde hair said. She gave a little wave and a kiss before giggling.

The redhead stood, looking bored and seductive at the same time as she smoked a cigarette. She said nothing. The woman with the book held it to her chest and waved. Her lips moved, but he couldn't hear her.

The multicolor-haired woman in a bikini danced around, her arms and legs moving as she twirled in circles even though there was no music.

"What's going on?" a mercenary yelled.

A loud whistle pierced the night.

"Hot damn! Is it my birthday already?" one of Milano's men yelled. "What are you doing out here, sweetheart?"

"We have a schedule to keep," an irritated voice added to the mix as a man came out of the driver's seat of the semi. He went toward the front vehicles.

Frost surged forward, running as fast as he could toward the back of the semi while the men were distracted. He searched the cargo door for a way to get in.

"Expecting a rescue, Elle?" a muffled voice inside the trailer mocked. She didn't answer. "Did you think you'd be able to hide your identity? From us? You have to have known we were coming, and you led us right to the jackpot."

Frost touched the back door. A metal latch at the bottom held it in place. He tugged the handle as hard as he could, prying it open. The door bounced up a little.

"What's going on?" Black shoes appeared through the narrow opening on the bottom of the door. "Why have we stopped?"

Frost reached under the door and grabbed the mercenary by his ankles. He pulled forward, jerking him off his feet. The man fell back with a loud smack and then started kicking.

Frost pushed open the door and leapt inside. Muffled words sounded like a warning, and he found Snow bound by his hands and hanging from the ceiling. Bruises and welts littered his body, some bleeding, some caked with dried blood, the blue smearing his altered flesh. The blue of his skin was reemerging.

A second guard came from the back of the trailer, stepping around stacks of boxes. He pulled a gun from his waist. A patch on his chest read "Garrett." Frost shoved the heel of his hand into Garrett's chest, knocking the air from him. He then struck the man's jaw. Garrett fell against Snow, who caught him with his legs. Snow hooked his ankles and held on tight.

The man on the ground caught Frost by the leg and tried to kick the back of his knees to knock him over. Frost stumbled before managing to land his foot against the man's temple.

Garrett dropped to the floor beneath Snow.

"Any more?" Frost asked.

Snow shook his head. A band of silver adhered to his mouth. Frost grabbed his brother by the legs and held him up while Snow unhooked the chain link of the cuffs from a hook on the ceiling. It took several attempts, but Snow finally managed to get free, and his weight dropped forward.

Snow landed on the floor and then used his cuffed hands to pry the band from his mouth. It stretched his skin, and he grunted in discomfort.

Frost rushed toward the back of the cargo area. A metal barrier with slits had been welded to the trailer wall to create a hidden cage. If not for the open door, he might have missed it. The rusted metal and worn lock acted as evidence that this was not the first transport the truck had made.

Ice was bound across from his wife. Frost set about freeing Elle.

Anger shone in her eyes, and she thrust her body forward several times to indicate she was trapped. Like Snow, she had a band across her mouth. Her hands were behind her back, and her wrists chained to the grate with a self-locking hook. Frost squeezed it, managing to set her free. Her hands were still bound behind her so she couldn't free her mouth to speak.

Commands sounded from the communication devices on the fallen men. "They're not real. It's a trick."

"Find where it's coming from!"

"Check the woods!"

"Check the prisoners!"

Frost unclipped his brother and reached to pull the band from his mouth. It was on tight, and he had to yank hard to rip it off. Ice's mouth opened as if to scream in pain, but no sound came out. He breathed hard and nodded his head. A dark blue mark showed on his face where the tape had been.

Frost glanced at Elle. She made a funny noise and jutted her jaw into the air a couple of times. He pretended not to understand. There was no way he would be the one to put her through that kind of pain.

"We have to go," Frost said. "They're coming, and there is a lot of them."

"You stupid bellaphant," Ice scolded in their shared Sintazian language. "What are you doing here? Now we'll all be captured."

"I couldn't leave you," Frost answered in kind. Before adding in English, "Jackass."

Elle pointed her hands toward the floor and bent as if she would try to reach something. With her hands behind her back, the movement was awkward. Seeing Meg's camera on the floor, Frost reached for it. The camera was evidence that Milano's men had been in their home.

"Let's go!" Snow ordered in a forceful whisper. He had freed himself and carried a set of keys. He slipped off the back of the trailer and then waved his hand for them to follow.

"Aliens," a woman screamed, "help, blue monsters!"

Meg? What was she doing here? Why was she helping Milano? Why was she calling him a monster? The word hit him harder than any punch ever could.

He hopped out of the trailer and looked for her.

"They're in the forest," Meg cried. "Please, help me, you have to come! There are five of them and...and...a green, scaly one!"

"Frost, help," Snow said under his breath.

Frost turned to help him support Elle and Ice as they came off the semi-truck with bound hands.

"What is wrong?" Snow asked him as he unlocked Elle's cuffs.

"Meg," Frost said.

"What about her?" Snow then went to free Ice.

"She's here," Frost answered.

"That was Meg yelling?" Ice asked. "What is she doing here?"

"I don't know why she would say I was a monster." Frost frowned. "I thought she liked me."

Elle pulled the band from her mouth. She slapped it hard against his t-shirt so that it stuck to him. "Next time, rip the tape off my mouth. I'm not a delicate flower and I like air."

He didn't remove the tape from his clothing. Next time? There had better never be a next time.

"Sometimes you Sintazians are too honest for

your own good. Meg didn't mean it. She called you guys monsters because she's trying to help us," Elle explained. She grabbed the camera from him and moved to the truck. "She lied to divert the men in the other direction so we could escape."

Elle lifted the camera, and a recording of the scene appeared on the back screen.

"We need to go," Ice said.

"Smile for the camera," Elle told the unconscious men. "Let's see how your boss likes this online video going viral." After recording the mercenaries, she got the side of the truck that had Milano's name on it.

"What are you doing?" Snow asked.

Elle pointed the camera around the other side of the truck toward the commotion while trying to stay out of sight. "Just making a little movie. They can't get away with this. Let's see Franky Milano try to explain this mess to—"

Running feet cut off her words, and she lifted her hand for silence and held still.

"Run," Ice ordered. Elle and Snow went after him

Frost waited until the others were almost to the trees before following. He listened for Meg but heard no more. He ducked into the cover of the trees.

"The prisoners have escaped," a mercenary shouted. They watched him from their hiding places as he searched around the truck. Elle pressed the back of the camera against her body while covering its indicator lights with her hands so no one would see it in the dark. She aimed it at the men. "They're in the forest!"

"I must find Meg," Frost whispered.

"What's the next part of your plan?" Ice pulled on Frost's arm to get his attention off looking for Meg.

"Bob and Gary are supposed to pick us up a few miles down the road." Frost gestured away from where he'd heard Meg's voice. "You get to the ship. I'm going—"

"Going to get yourself killed?" Elle interrupted. "I know these men. They took me because I was one of them and I know better, but Meg is a civilian. They will have no reason to harm her. At worst, they'll feed her some cover story to make her feel like she's crazy. When I worked for the foundation, they had specific orders we had to follow. Civilian injuries equal exposure. Milano values his reputation above all other things. He's a vain prick."

Her assurances did not ease Frost's worry.

They heard a crunch in the forest. In unison, they turned toward the sound. Snow motioned to the side. Frost nodded. They waited, listening to the movement. Suddenly, Snow jumped. Frost followed. Snow thrust the flat of his hand to a mercenary's throat so he couldn't yell for help. The man fell back. Frost hooked his arm around the man's neck and squeezed as Elle had shown them. The move worked, and the attacker fell limp. He was unconscious but alive.

"If you stay, I stay," Snow told Frost.

"No one is staying," Ice commanded. "We all go."

Frost placed his fist against Ice's shoulder. "I love her."

Ice took a deep breath and gave him a look of understanding. "Then we will come back for her. I promise. Right now, there are too many of them to fight."

Frost hesitated but ultimately nodded. "The ship is that way."

Ice took Elle's hand and ran with her down the side of the road as fast as he could. Tree limbs cast shadows, hiding them from view, but they wouldn't be safe out in the open for long. His brother needed to get his wife to safety. Snow waited for Frost. They began running after them. Frost slowed his pace. When Snow moved ahead of him and was distracted by Ice motioning for them to take cover in the trees, Frost darted the other direction and entered the woods. He would not risk his family now that they were free from Milano, but he would not leave Meg behind.

12

MEG WATCHED THE ARMED MEN CREATE A protective formation around her as they pushed through the trees. These weren't hacks. They were well trained and, if the array of weapons they carried was any indication, they were deadly. She knew the instant she saw them they meant business. And that business would be capturing or killing aliens.

Meg had to do something to help Frost, and it was the most terrifying thing she'd ever done. Thankfully, her shaking could be construed as fear of aliens when, in truth, she was frightened by the kind of people who would kidnap and transport them in the dead of night.

The journalist in her knew she was on the

cusp of a world-changing story—Milano Foundation acting as a front for alien mercenaries, the kidnapping of Elle, and the biggest question about the universe finally answered. Aliens were real. Earth was not alone.

There would never be a bigger story, but to tell it, she would have to expose Frost and his family. The cost for them would be great.

For once in her life, the writer part of her was drowned out by a desire to be cautious—protect Frost, keep his secret, help his family.

Jumping in front of a transport of armed men might have been the bravest thing she'd ever done...and most likely the stupidest. Every time she tried to hold back or sneak away, one of them would come from the shadows and block her path. It became quickly apparent that they were keeping a close eye on her. She thought about running, but could she outrun a trained soldier with a gun, let alone a half dozen mercenaries?

Spaceship teleportation sounded good about right now.

A ripple of commands went through the men, including one that said the prisoners had escaped. Meg held her breath, searching the darkness like the rest of them. The longer they kept looking, the more relieved she felt. It meant they hadn't found them. Frost had succeeded. He was safe and would soon be on his way home.

That thought caused a tear to run down her cheek. She should have said more to him after that last kiss. She should have said she wanted to see him again. She should have said they'd find a way, at least to give themselves a chance. The ache inside her chest became unbearable.

Meg took a step back. They had gone too far, too deep into the woods. No one would hear her screams out here. She needed to find a way to get free.

A hand grabbed her by the arm, holding tight. Meg tried to pull away from...

Her eyes went to the patch on his chest. She tried to pull away from Spencer. He wouldn't release her.

"How far did you run?" There was no gentleness in his touch or his voice, and his green eyes were narrowed with a barely contained anger. She had seen that look before in people she'd interviewed while living in Chicago. Normally, they were behind a plastic barricade in prison for some kind of violent crime.

None of your business, she thought, only to answer aloud, “I don’t know.”

“What were you doing out here?”

Distracting you.

“I don’t know.”

By his expression, these answers were not what he wanted to hear. His grip tightened painfully. “How did you get here?”

Spaceship.

“I can’t remember.”

“Do you have anything to say for yourself?”

You’re an asshole.

“You’re an asshole.”

Oh, shit, I shouldn’t have said that.

Spencer’s eyes narrowed. His fingers squeezed so hard that it caused her to cry out in pain. He jerked her violently, and her knees buckled as he forced her to the ground. She clawed at his hand.

“What’s going on?” A ponytailed man appeared.

“She’s hiding something, sir,” Spencer said. Meg cried out again as his fingers shifted their tight hold. “There’s no one out here. We should have found something by now.”

Sir turned his back and said something into the speaker microphone clipped on his shoulder.

"Air support is two minutes out," came a crackling answer.

"Report," Sir ordered, to which the answers came:

"West, negative."

"Nothing on the east."

"South, nothing."

Sir kept his hand on the two-way, waiting for another answer. When no other report came in, he said, "North?"

Nothing.

"North, report," he ordered gruffly. "Garrett? Erickson? Report, now."

Silence.

"All teams north!" Sir ordered into the mic. He gave her an aggravated look and said to Spencer, "Lock her up for now. We'll deal with her later."

Spencer hauled her to her feet and forced her through the forest with him, taking her in the direction of the lead truck while the other dispersed toward the semi. His expression become openly hostile now that they were left alone.

"Let me go," Meg ordered. Running from one would be easier than a whole squad of gun-toting mercs. "You have no right to detain me. I didn't do anything. I—"

Spencer smacked her across the cheek, hard. "Shut up."

She moaned as her head snapped to the side. Shocked, she touched her throbbing cheek. She tasted blood where her teeth cut the inside of her lip. The bastard had hit her.

Fuck you, asshole. You're not taking me to some secret facility.

Meg screamed at the top of her lungs and flung her fist toward his face. She didn't care what she struck or how, she just lobbed everything she had. She kicked, she kneed, she punched his neck, she scratched flesh. When his grip on her arm loosened, she ripped herself free and struck him with that hand as well. Instructions came through his comm.

She lunged at him with all she had. He punched her shoulder, but it only fueled her rage. Adrenaline pumped through her. He stumbled as her weight hit him and he fell. Meg didn't quit her assault. She only knew she had to stop him if she wanted a chance at freedom.

She landed on him and threw her elbow into his throat. He gasped even as he shoved her off him. Meg landed on her back. She rolled and crawled to get away. Spencer grabbed her by the ankle and pulled her through the dirt back to him.

Meg kicked and blindly reached out as she tried to find something to hold on to. The pain of his blows crept in, replacing the adrenaline. With each passing second, she felt worse.

"Spencer, why didn't you—*shit!*"

Meg's hand wrapped around a booted ankle and she instantly let go. There were too many mercenaries running around the forest. She was a fool to think she could escape them. Spencer dragged her toward him, pawing her legs.

"Fuck you, assholes. At least you didn't get them," she whispered.

13

FROST FOLLOWED THE SOUND OF MEG'S CRIES. Elle had been wrong. They were hurting her. If he hadn't tried to blend in by playing hockey, none of this would be happening—Meg would never have come after him, and she'd be safe. It had sounded as if Milano had tracked Elle, but it could have just as easily been because of him. The guilt ate at him, but also made him determined to do something about it. He would fix this mistake.

"You heard the boss, to the north," a man yelled.

Frost slowed his pace and ducked behind a tree as a group of mercenaries moved past. When they disappeared into the forest, he again moved toward Meg.

A hand clamped on his shoulder and he turned, fingers spread as he prepared to punch whoever was there with the palm of his hand.

"Easy," Snow whispered, releasing him. "I told you, I wouldn't let you come alone."

Frost searched the surrounding forest for Ice.

"He's taking Elle to the ship," Snow said. "Come on. Let's rescue your bride."

Frost had never said Meg was his bride, but he felt no need to correct his brother. He liked the sound of it. As he continued through the forest, listening for any sign she was near, he heard the steady pulse of Snow's feet behind him. The speed did not allow for stealth, but he could not waste time.

He wasn't sure how he found her in the chaos of what was happening, but his instincts seemed to know where he needed to go. An invisible force called to his heart, joining it to hers. He did not question the feeling. This is what being in love was. Meg was his forever. He knew that as sure as he knew anything.

He found Meg on the ground crawling away from someone who tried to pull her back. The attacker was also on his stomach. They both looked pretty beaten up. A second man with blond hair reached for her wrist. Frost didn't check for other dangers as he reacted. He charged at the standing soldier and leapt at the man like he was attacking a rabid bearguar.

His shoulder slammed the mercenary in the chest. The terrain wasn't like fighting on ice, and he did not slide as much as he was used to when he landed. It didn't matter. The man was hurting Meg. For that, he would pay dearly.

"Frost." Her voice was small, but he heard her say his name. She grunted, and he saw her kick her attacker in the face. "Let," *kick*, "me," *kick*, "go, asshole."

Frost circled the blond mercenary. Snow appeared to help Meg. He pulled her from the ground before turning to face the bloodied attacker.

The blond tried to pull a gun from his waist, but Frost didn't give him the chance to use it. He hit the man's chest in a rapid succession of palm thrusts. When the mercenary dropped the weapon, Frost swept a palm to his face, knocking him on his back. He didn't move.

"Meg." He rushed to her side.

Snow nudged the man she'd kicked. "Well done, sister."

"Frost." She let him come to her as she lifted her arms a few inches to welcome him. Meg trembled in his embrace. A sob broke free from her. "He hit me. I thought they were going to..."

"I will never let harm befall you, my love, I promise." Frost held her closer.

"Frost, we need to go. The ship is waiting," insisted Snow.

Meg made no effort to move. He wasn't sure she could at the moment. Frost swept her into his arms and carried her. He nodded at Snow to lead the way. Meg wrapped her arms around his neck.

"They're going after you; north, I mean," Meg said. The sound of a helicopter zoomed overhead, shining a bright beam of light over the forest. Frost had seen the flying machines on television. She looked up at the sky. "They called in air support."

"We'll never make it back to the ship," Snow said. "We'll have to travel in the other direction."

"Go," Frost agreed. "Gary put locator chips inside us. They'll be able to track us down. All we have to do is find a safe place to wait."

14

THE INSIDE OF A RUNDOWN REST STOP WASN'T exactly the ideal place to sleep, but Meg couldn't complain. Her entire body felt either bruised, bloodied, or sprained. The hard tile floor and wall didn't help, and she shifted but was unable to get comfortable. A fluorescent light buzzed, a loud constant behind the dripping of water. The air was stale, laced with the odor of cheap cleaner and dust. The pressure of Frost's arm around her hurt, but she didn't want him to release her. She'd endure anything for just a few more moments with him.

The worst pain of all though came from her heart. How could she let Frost go?

Even if she didn't have her father to think

about, she couldn't go with him. If Sintaz were like the Arctic, she wouldn't last long. Scientists with all their equipment and snowsuits and training didn't stay in that environment all year round.

It was too dangerous for Frost to stay behind. She would never ask him to do it. She had seen the men Milano had sent after the Sintazian brothers.

Snow's gaze met hers. His skin had become a strange shade of tan tinged with enough blue to be noticeable. He gave her a small smile. "You defended yourself well, little one."

Meg couldn't help smirking at the nickname. "Thank you, big one."

"Hey," Frost protested. "I am your big one."

"No, you are my only one," Meg said before she could think to stop herself. However, now said, she found she didn't care. "You called me *my love*. Did you mean it? Am I your love?"

Snow made a strange noise and stood. "I will walk the perimeter."

Frost cupped her cheek. "How can you even ask me that? How can you not feel that thread between us? Of course you are my love. You are my forever. I never thought it was possible, but as

I look at you, every tribulation on this planet has been worth it." He brushed a tear that slid down her cheek. "Why do you cry?"

"Because you can't stay, and I can't go." Another tear fell. She was tired, sore, and heart-broken. It made for a messy combination of emotions. "I don't want you to go."

"Then I won't," he stated. "I will stay. For you. With you."

"But that can't work. You saw the lengths those men will go through to capture all of you. It's not safe for you here." Meg forgot her injuries as she moved to better face him in the dim light. "I don't want you to go, but it would kill me to see you hurt."

The fact that she meant every word, knew them to be true after such a short time was amazing.

A hint of orange light peeked into the window, signaling that dawn was finally near.

Snow came running into the restroom. "They're here. Hurry."

Frost hesitated to follow his brother. He cupped Meg's cheek. "Then we have a problem, my love. If I leave you that will kill *me*."

"Frost, the ship," Snow insisted.

Before Meg could speak, Frost had stood and pulled her up next to him. "Do you want me to carry you?"

Her legs did, but the rest of her was too sore to be held. She shook her head. "I can walk."

"They'll be able to help you heal on the ship." He studied her face, and she knew he was looking at her bruises. When they'd first entered, she'd gotten a glimpse of what she looked like in the mirror. It wasn't pretty yet Frost still managed to gaze at her like she was the most beautiful thing he'd seen in all the universe.

They followed Snow behind the building. Meg limped next to Frost. The ship had landed at an odd angle, wedged up against some cracked trees and a brick storage shed. The door was open, and Ice stood in the entryway waving his hand for them to hurry.

Meg's legs weakened. Frost lifted her and ran the rest of the way. When he neared Ice, he asked, "Is Elle safe?"

"Yes. She's here." Ice's eyes rounded when he saw Meg. "What did they do to her?"

"Elle was wrong. They would hurt an Earth woman," Snow said.

"But you should see the face of the guy who did it," Frost said. "Meg clearly won that battle."

"Strap her in," Ice said. "We will have Gary heal her as soon as we're out of here. They have the medical device the Reticulans gave them."

Elle was already strapped into a seat. She took one look at Meg and gasped. "Milano's men did that? Do you know who?"

"Spencer," Meg said. "And some blond one."

"I don't know a Spencer. They must be recruiting." Elle's frown deepened. "And evidently they're not being as picky with their hiring practices as they once were."

Meg didn't answer as Frost set her down by the seats. She let him strap her in and then waited as he sat next to her. She grabbed his hand and gazed into his eyes while they took off. "I love you, Frost. I don't want you to go. I want to find a way for it to work."

"And I love you," Frost answered. He grinned widely and said over her shoulder, "Do you hear that?"

"Well done, brother," Snow said. "I am pleased for you."

"I wish you much happiness and many children," Ice added, nodding in approval.

Meg gave Elle a confused look.

"Congratulations," Elle drawled with a small laugh.

"What?" Meg asked.

"According to Sintazian customs, you just got married," Elle answered.

"Wait, how?" She looked around at the three brothers.

"You have chosen to be with him," Snow said.

"You have spoken words of love," Ice added.

"And we have come together for the Earth sex," Frost announced. He pointed at the chair they had used during their lovemaking. "Right there." He then pointed to where he'd first penetrated her. "And there."

Meg gasped, unable to believe he had announced a private moment like that.

Elle sighed and gave her an expression of comradery. "Yeah, they kind of have no filters with each other. You'll learn to get used to it. They also like to walk around naked. A lot. And they don't always knock before coming into each other's bedrooms, which is weird when it's also *your* bedroom. I've been working on assimilating them to Earth ways. It hasn't been a fast process."

"Was the Earth sex as Ice described it?" Snow asked. "You moved the hips?"

Meg tried to protest, but all that came out was a strangled noise.

"Yes." Frost gave a big nod. "It is very pleasurable. I will do it again many, many times as soon as my wife is healed."

The ship shook as it began takeoff. The jarring reminded Meg of her sore body, and she closed her eyes. Taking a deep breath, she whispered, "Frost, I love you, and I will gladly be your wife, but if they try to watch us have sex—"

A metal clang cut off her words as the ship propelled into the air like a bad carnival ride. She kept her eyes closed and held her breath. Meg couldn't decide what was crazier—the fact she was flying into space on a ship or the fact she'd married a blue alien and couldn't be happier.

15

EPILOGUE

MEG GRINNED AT THE COMPUTER SCREEN, pleased with herself as she stared at the op-ed piece she'd posted about Milano. A little research, when she knew what she was looking for, had been enough to cause speculation. The video that Elle had shot, with a little editing, supported the piece. The comments people made were mostly rumors and innuendos, but the beauty (and the curse) of the internet was that facts weren't always what it took to get a good tale to go viral.

That's all Meg needed—for this story to get going. Elle swore Milano was the type of man who valued his secrecy almost as much as his need to be seen as a good guy in the public's eyes. If people started questioning the Milano Foundation, then they would dig deeper. Milano would be put under a public microscope. It wouldn't necessarily stop him, but it could hamper his plans. Plus, video evidence of shady dealings was hard to dispute. People loved a good intrigue, and the thing had almost a half million views after only a few days. The next step would be to keep the story going and in front of the public's eyes.

"Look, I am human," Frost announced, coming into her father's living room.

Meg turned to study her husband. His face was painted a dark tan with a thick theater makeup, and his hair had been cut into an edgier style. It spiked up on the top in a structured mess.

Jenny Mirani came up behind him. Her long dress and beaded vest made her look as if she'd just walked out of the 1970s. The woman had insisted Meg call her Jenny. After all, it turned out her father had finally proposed to the woman while Meg was on her little adventure, and they were to be family. Her father looked so happy, and that was all Meg needed to know. Jenny would be a good wife and would take care of him.

"Where are the onions?" her father called from the kitchen.

"In the bin, Jerry," Jenny answered.

It took her father a little more time to come to terms with Meg's blue husband, but when he saw how happy she was, he accepted her decision. Facing a life-threatening illness tended to put things in perspective. All her father wanted was for Meg to be happy. Life could be short, and time was precious.

"Told ya I would make him look human," Jenny said.

"That's amazing," Meg admitted. It wasn't perfect, at least not enough to pass scrutiny, but for their purposes it would work.

All they needed were a few pictures with the hockey players to go with her article. Billy Weaver had been so excited about Frost rejoining the Voyageurs that he was only too willing to have the entire team paint themselves blue for each game. Blue was the color of a first-place ribbon and thus perfect for his team, he had decided. With a couple of photos of Frost in a more human skin tone and the rumors of a blue man playing hockey would be nothing more than a small-town quirk. It wouldn't stop Milano, but it would help keep their secret from the rest of the world.

"Did I ever tell you about the time I saw a flying saucer?" Jenny asked, tapping Frost's arm.

He shook his head in denial. "Well, it was about 1977, thereabouts, and we were camping in the woods outside Pondue. When, all of a sudden, during the middle of our campfire singalong comes what we thought was a shooting star, but then this bright light shone down from the sky. It nearly burned the eyes out of my head."

"Jenny, where are the peppers?" Meg's father yelled.

"In the bin," Jenny answered.

Frost frowned. "I have never heard of a spaceship that bright. Were you looking at thrusters? Though I'm not sure how you could see that brightness without being burnt to a crisp."

"It was life changing," Jenny said.

"Were you smoking copious amounts of pot?" Meg asked.

"It was the seventies." Jenny shrugged as if that was answer enough. "But I have to ask. Why are aliens taking humans? Is it to experiment on them? The anal probing thing, is that something aliens like to do or are those people whack jobs?"

Frost looked to Meg for help. She didn't step in.

"The only aliens I know taking humans is for wives," Frost said. "You are highly compactible with other humanoid species. It is why I came here to find Meg."

"I think the word you mean is compatible," Meg corrected.

"No, the hologram advertisement said you are compactible." Frost reached for her with a teasing grin.

"That is so romantic," Jenny said. Then, clapping her hands, she asked, "Who's hungry? I'm teaching your father how to make a casserole! You should eat before you head back to your new place. Wait, did he say peppers?"

Jenny didn't wait for an answer as she went to the kitchen.

Their new place was an old farm about fifteen miles outside town. Jenny owned the land, but no one had lived there for years. It had solar panels, well water, and a generator, but that was about it. The cabin home was as far off the grid as they would find without leaving the area. They all understood the risks. It wasn't safe, but it would do for now. Meg could only hope that Gary and Bob found a way to stop Milano so they could live in peace.

Elle and Meg had spent the better part of the last two weeks installing security cameras and motion sensors around the property. Their cellphone internet connection was spotty, so Meg had to come to her father's house to get any kind of work done online.

Meg wrapped her arms around Frost. "Elle's video is getting traction, that's good."

"Ice called and told me that Elle's parents are safe. They reported the guesthouse break-in to the police. Bob and Gary are monitoring the situation, and there has been no mention of you on any channels. They don't know who you are. Galaxy Brides is also tracking Franky Milano. They say they have a plan, but they have not said what that plan is."

"Can we trust them?" Meg didn't like the human color on her husband. Though he was handsome no matter what, it didn't look like him. "They haven't been very truthful so far."

"I don't think they meant to lie, so much as they neglected to tell the whole truth." He touched a finger to her brow and massaged lightly to get her to stop furrowing it. "The company they work for wants these trips to work. It is in Gary and Bob's best interest to see to it this planet is safe. If anything happens to us, the Federation could shut them down."

"They better keep you safe," Meg said. "Or the Federation will be the least of their worries."

"I love you, too." Frost pressed his mouth to hers in a deep kiss.

The future might be unknown, but it was not uncertain. This was the life she was always meant to have. Adventure. Frost. Love.

The sound of Jenny's singing broke through the trance of his mouth. Her father's voice joined in. The song was not in tune.

She laughed as she pulled away. "I'm going to finish checking a few things before we leave. Why don't you go sweet-talk Jenny into sending food home with us? One thing is for sure, the woman can cook."

Frost nodded. He went to the kitchen. "Jenny, I am to sweet-talk food from you for my family."

Meg laughed and shook her head at his bluntness. Frost was definitely one adventure she didn't mind having.

The End

THE SERIES

Galaxy Alien Mail Order Brides Series

Spark

Flame

Blaze

Ice

Frost

Snow

KEEP READING!

SNOW

Galaxy Alien Mail Order Brides Book 6

Alpha male alien comes to Earth to pick up a bride and instead meets a beautiful scientist whose job it is to capture him.

NYT Bestselling Author, Michelle M. Pillow, is back with a brand new sci-fi alien romance adventure.

Tushar (aka Snow Chaos) knows there is little chance of finding a wife on his ice-ball of a home planet. Few can survive the subzero temperatures. When Galaxy Alien Mail Order Brides offers to introduce them to women eager for love, he and his brothers can't resist, but Earth is far from welcoming.

He knows he should focus on getting home, but all he can think about is laying claim to the sexy scientist who works for the bad guys.

Jennifer works for the Milano Foundation in an attempt to undermine their efforts. When Snow and his brothers land, it's like a dream come true for her diabolical alien-kidnapping coworkers. Now she has to make a choice--keep her cover, or betray a dangerous corporation to save the alien she's falling in love with.

Snow might be a blue humanoid from another planet, but life with him might be worth the risk.

Length: Long Novella/Short Novel

Contemporary Alien Science Fiction Fantasy Paranormal Romance

A Qurilixen World Novella

ABOUT THE AUTHOR

New York Times* & *USA TODAY
Bestselling Author

Michelle loves to travel and try new things, whether it's a paranormal investigation of an old Vaudeville Theatre or climbing Mayan temples in Belize. She believes life is an adventure fueled by copious amounts of coffee.

Newly relocated to the American South, Michelle is involved in various film and documentary projects with her talented director husband. She is mom to a fantastic artist. And she's managed by a dog and cat who make sure she's meeting her deadlines.

For the most part she can be found wearing pajama pants and working in her office. There may or may not be dancing. It's all part of the creative process.

Come say hello! Michelle loves talking with readers on social media!

www.MichellePillow.com

facebook.com/AuthorMichellePillow

twitter.com/michellepillow

instagram.com/michellempillow

bookbub.com/authors/michelle-m-pillow

goodreads.com/Michelle_Pillow

amazon.com/author/michellepillow

youtube.com/michellepillow

pinterest.com/michellepillow

READING GUIDES

MICHELLE M. PILLOW NOVELS

Free Reading Guides

Download free reading guides in MOBI or EPUB formats from MichellePillow.com.

COMPLIMENTARY EXCERPTS

TRY BEFORE YOU BUY!

IF YOU ENJOYED THIS SERIES...

Space Lords: His Frost Maiden by Michelle M. Pillow

Empath and space pirate, Evan Cormier is obsessed with decoding an ominous premonition about his future. When a fellow crewman angered a spirit, the vengeful Zhang An took her wrath out on everyone in the vicinity. Evan just happened to be one of them. He's now facing a future in which he'll be forever alone.

Lady Josselyn of the House of Craven has been betrayed. With her home world on a Florencian moon under attack and her family dead, she finds herself at the mercy of the one who deceived them. There is only one thing left to do—die with honor. But before she can join her family in the afterlife, she must first avenge all that she held dear. Falling in love with a pirate was never in the plan. Evan and his thieving crewmates might have delayed her fate, but they can't stop destiny.

His Frost Maiden Excerpt

Craven Estates, Earth Settlement, Florencia's Fifth Moon

"Lift her," the General ordered, his shiny boots walking away from her, taking her reflection with it.

Two men hauled her to her feet, holding her up by her arms. Josselyn suppressed a cry as they jerked her dislocated shoulder. She couldn't see their faces, didn't need to. Her body hurt so badly she couldn't tell where the pain was coming from anymore.

The one who'd betrayed them stood before her. General Jack Stephans. He'd deceived her family and the fifth moon settlement. He'd traded them in for money and power. Josselyn lifted her gaze briefly to the hard depths of the steel green eyes before her. She wanted to kick, to give one last good blow, to go down fighting, but she couldn't raise her limbs.

"Poor little Josselyn, so heartbreaking," the General grabbed her chin and swiped beneath her eye. He looked young, was in fact very young for his position, only a few years older than her six and twenty. And yet they all knew so much more of fighting than anyone their age should, than anyone ever should.

"We gave you a home," she whispered. "How could you do this? How could you join them?"

"You gave me a place in your stables," he spat, his grip tightening on her chin, bruisingly so. "Not a place at your table. Not a place by your side. Not equal. They gave me a rank, a title. They give me respect. They give me a place in this world."

"Jack," she said, her voice softening for the orphan boy they'd found over twenty years ago. If she begged him, maybe fate could be turned around; maybe this day could be erased. Fate had spit them out in a whirlwind of chance and deceit. Maybe all that had happened wasn't his fault. Maybe it wasn't hers. None of it mattered. None of it changed the fact that he had taken everything she held dear, everyone, and now he was robbing her of her family home. Her tone hardened and she closed her eyes. "General."

"Look at me, Josselyn," he said. His tone caught even as his grip on her face tightened until his fingers pressed the inside of her cheeks against her teeth. "You're so cold. Even now, your face is composed. Is one, lonely tear all the passion you can muster?"

"I am Lady Josselyn of the House of Craven." Her eyes opened slowly, focusing on the shiny white of his uniform. It gleamed with the orange glow coming from the fireplace. The material looked odd in the drabber earth tones many on the fifth moon wore. Theirs was a world based on Medieval Earth. Each moon in the Florencian system was different, each settlement patterned off a singular time in the human past, times that history had almost forgotten. But the principals of the ancestors who'd established the colonies no longer applied. Times were different now. What had started as preservation of history had turned into reality, into laws and a way of life they all believed in as generation after generation was raised into the worlds of the Florencian moons.

The General shook her by the face until finally she forced her eyes to meet his. He looked angry, hurt, wildly hopeful. "I can save you. I can say you had nothing to do with the treachery of your family. No one wants to kill a woman of noble blood. The line of Craven doesn't have to die. I will take your name; the name denied me by your father."

Was he serious? She knew he'd asked her father for her hand in marriage. In fact, she'd dismissed the proposal with the full knowledge he only asked because he wanted power. Did he think she could love him now? Want him? Take him into her bed?

He must have read the answer on her face because his own expression hardened. She knew Jack. He wouldn't ask again.

"I suppose not," he said, almost sad. "Even if you agreed, I could never trust you not to take a blade to my back. Not after today." He sighed heavily. "Not after this."

"Ago," she whispered, even her voice beginning to fail in its strength, "pugna quod int-"

"Quiet your tongue! This house is mine. Mine." He let go of her chin and her head drooped. "And you can die knowing that I have taken more than what you all refused to give me in life."

"A place at our table," Josselyn said, her tone softer still, the will to live leaving her. Her heart called out to her ancestors, to her dead family, begging them to come and get her.

"My table," he answered, stepping away. The General lifted a gun, pointing it at her head. She heard the telltale click of metal on metal. The weapon was not one found on the fifth moon. They fought with swords and axes, like the old medieval ways. Though technology was available, not using it was a point of honor. He must have brought the weapon from another moon. Perhaps the Victorians? The Elizabethans? It appeared to be too old to be from much later in time.

"Do it, Jack." She didn't look at him as she waited for the final discharge of the gun, the loud bang before the end. When it didn't come, she repeated, the words a mere mouthing of her lips, "Do it."

"Speed you to a quick end, Josselyn Craven," Jack whispered. "You all brought this on yourselves."

www.MichellePillow.com

Space Lords Series

His Frost Maiden
His Fire Maiden
His Metal Maiden
His Earth Maiden
His Woodland Maiden

PILLOW FIGHTER FAN CLUB!

FAN OF MICHELLE M. PILLOW?

Want to join an awesome group of readers?
facebook.com/groups/MichellePillowFanClub

PLEASE LEAVE A REVIEW

THANK YOU FOR READING!

Please take a moment to share your thoughts by reviewing this book.

Be sure to check out Michelle's other titles at www.MichellePillow.com

www.ingramcontent.com/pod-product-compliance
Lightning Source LLC
Chambersburg PA
CBHW030635120726
47904CB00006B/2155

9781625012197